Differently Double

By Susan Murray-Miller

An Emeryville Murder Mystery

Copyright 2021 by Susan Murray-Miller

Edited by Sarah Harrer - Sarah Harrer Proofs

Published by Plaide Palette Publishing
Cherry Valley, NY 13320

First Edition Paperback
ISBN 978-0-9746558-5-7

To Jeffrey...memories of you will forever be in our hearts and our thoughts.

Welcome to Emeryville, New York where nothing is as it seems on the surface and home is not a physicality, but a state of mind.

Prologue

He was a drifter, a wanderer, a killer. His innocence had been taken from him at an early age by women his father had hooked up with. He was used to the hotel rooms, the trailers and the shacks where they temporarily set up housekeeping. But always, there was that terrible fight and then his father would turn from a mild-mannered, poor excuse for a human being into a thing of rage and destruction. They would leave in the middle of the night after disposing of the body in an out-of-the-way spot. "Bury it deep and the dogs won't find it," is all his father would say to him. Now, always alone and wandering, he searched for a soul he never knew he had and a past he had to erase.

August

Chapter One

The local riding stable summer lesson program was in full swing. Entourages of horses and riders could be seen on the village streets walking past the bank in the early morning hours and in the roads at the opposite end of the village during the afternoons.

The mayor, obsessed with clean streets and sidewalks, took his usual exception, but most folks just let bygones be bygones. This was a *right to farm* community after all and for the most part if you wanted to live here amongst the beauty and the blessed peace, you put up with the occasional smells and leftovers from the local dairy and goat farms and the riding academy. It was bad enough having to dodge logging trucks with their cargo of logs headed for the local mills during the late fall and winter months, so a little manure wasn't considered a big deal.

Dottie, owner of the local riding academy and boarding facility, was leading a group of twelve in an intermediate trail ride. It was 7:00 am on this bright, cool morning. Dottie was riding her mount of choice, Ferd. Following close behind was Ferd's sidekick, Valerie.

Little Hannah held onto Valerie's reins tightly, her helmet strapped securely to her head and her eyes wide with anticipation of the gallop in the fields just outside the village limits.

Dottie had warned Hannah about Valerie and told her of Valerie's infatuation with the owner of a particular house on Main Street. Whenever Valerie passed this particular house she would prance, nicker and sidestep and basically make a horsey fool of herself for everyone to see.

"Watch her closely or she'll go to visit. Just keep her on course," she told the little girl. "Don't take any bull from her."

Hannah could feel Valerie tense with excitement as they approached the particular house. It was almost like her behavior when they passed the bakery just a few blocks back and the patrons had all waved and shouted as they rode past. Of course, Valerie and Ferd had to resort to their prancing as the patrons waved as they walked past.

"I think they think they're getting donuts. Not!" muttered Dottie as she waved and smiled.

Walking placidly across the bridge and past the cemetery, the group turned onto the dirt road that would put them into large meadows and fields awash with grasses, legumes and wildflowers. Here, one could ride at a full gallop and feel the wind in their face.

Chapter Two

Tom Pederson, owner of the local junkyard, stood in front of Amy Goodwin's desk. Amy was the principal of the Emeryville Public School and Tom was looking into the prospects of enrolling his only son, Alex, in school for the first time in many years.

"Well, Mr. Pederson," Amy said, "I understand you want to speak with me."

"Need to enroll my son in school," he said gruffly.

"About time, don't you think?" said Amy, casually eyeing him from over the top of her bright red glasses that perched on the end of her nose. "The last time he was in school was the year your wife passed, am I right? That was a long time ago. It's a wonder you aren't in jail or at least had a visit from a truant officer."

"Whatever. I know I made mistakes, but that's all in the past. Let's move on. I want him to at least finish school. Something I never did."

"Agreed, let's move on," said Amy cheerfully. "I understand, or more like it's rumored, that he's very good at basketball?"

"If they say so," mumbled Tom.

"Sit down, Tom." She motioned to the empty chair beside her desk. Amy knew Tom's penchant for eruption at a moment's notice, so she tried to keep the conversation light - very light.

"What does your son want?" she inquired. "He should be in the twelfth grade."

"Damned if I know," said Tom, nervously fingering the battered baseball cap in his hand.

"I would really like to speak with him one on one first. Then we'll go from there," she said. "Ok?"

Tom nodded and Amy continued. "Meanwhile, please fill out these papers. If you have any questions, just let me know."

A few minutes passed and Amy asked, "When can I see your son? There's about three more weeks left before school starts so maybe we can arrange something. I know you're shorthanded at the yard, and personally his work experience can't go unnoticed either. Anyway, I have to place him and the best thing for me to do now is to have a meeting with him."

"I'll get him in here tomorrow, if that's ok," sighed Tom.

Amy nodded as Tom got up and walked out the door.

Sad, she thought, how things can go so wrong and yet they could, possibly, end up so right.

The morning after his father's visit to the school, Alex was shown to Amy's office. He was in clean jeans, a tee shirt and sneakers. He was thin with a mop of unruly hair. He had grease stains on his hands belying the fact that he worked with cars and engines. When Amy addressed him, she noticed his stutter. As soon as he started to stutter, he would hesitate, take a deep breath and start to talk again. This time with better diction.

"Has someone been coaching you? Helping you with your stuttering?" Amy asked directly. Amy was not one for beating around the bush.

He nodded. "Lydia and Olivia, two friends of mine sa- sa- said that their ma- ma- mom has a client who stutters real bad and has been helped by new ways to address the problem," he said slowly. "When I rush or get excited, I get real bad."

Amy nodded, "I see," she said. Karen Bell, a local healer and Reiki master, was Lydia's mother. Lydia's best friend was Olivia. The dynamic duo, Amy labeled the two of them. Olivia's brother Josh worked weekends and summers with Alex at Pederson's Junk Yard and both boys had formed a bond. Josh was the captain of the basketball team.

"I'm going to have to give you a series of tests to see where I can place you. In the High School or BOCES or some other curriculum. How much can you read?" asked Amy.

"I read real well and I can do math and I know history," said Alex.

"How? You haven't been to school in years," said Amy, her eyes narrowing.

"I have help. My da- da- dad didn't know, but I got library books and I study and read. I used to get ho- hold of his newspapers, whenever I could."

"I'm intrigued," said Amy looking quizzically at her subject.

"There's a box by the main gate to the shop," he said slowly. "Claire, the librarian puts books in there for me. I read them and Pete, our hired man, used to take them back for me. Now, I go myself, after all the things happened here last year. After Pete died and all," he said quietly.

"Ok, tell you what, I'm going to try you in the ninth grade. I'll give you some questions in all subjects. If you pass, we'll go up the ladder from there until I'm satisfied. You should be in the twelfth grade along with Josh and his cohorts. Josh knows what he wants in life and it certainly isn't college. That's his decision. But you, what do you want in life?"

"I never thought of it. In the beginning just getting away from ma- ma- my father and the lousy house I was in. But now things have changed. I love my work. I like where I am and I'm beginning to find new friends, thanks to Josh and his friends."

"Alright," said Amy, pursing her lips, "today is Monday. Can you get off work say ...three o'clock on Friday? I'll give you a test here and then we'll go forward from that point. I don't think you would want a Regents curriculum; that's not needed now. I'm not saying you are or aren't college material. Right now, I have to get you placed in a grade where you belong."

~

Alex walked back to the junkyard and was met by Josh.

"Well, three on Friday is ma- ma- my first exam. Ninth grade."

"Wow," said Josh. "Let's get you some help."

"I really feel I want to just go for my GED and get the whole school thing over with," said Alex, slowly.

"What about basketball?" said Josh.

"I'll see if I can play and how many hours I'd have to put in. I'd have to have coaching on it. I've never played with a group. I watch it some on TV. My da- dad watches it sometimes," he said.

"Hey, by the way, new man coming on," said Josh.

"Yeah, with me in school and all and no more Pete, Dad does need more help. We're here on weekends, so maybe this guy can fill in during the da- days I'm in school. Have you seen him? He's the guy with the three kids."

"Oh, the one who's moved in across the street from Eugenia and Dottie. That rundown house with all the shutters missing?" asked Josh.

"It needs a coat of paint, that's all," said Alex. "It looks like a sound house and all."

"People say it's haunted," said Josh, excitedly.

"I'm sure if it was, Father from the Catholic Church would be there," Alex said quietly.

"No seriously, they say it's haunted," said Josh excitedly. "Remember that guy who committed suicide in there?"

Alex shook his head and said, "Yeah, heard about it, but that happened before ma- ma- my time."

Chapter Three

The Fosters, new people in town, arrived with pickup trucks and a moving van. People had gathered to help out with moving into the house on Maiden Lane. Charlie Foster was Tom's new employee, replacing Alex while he was in school. Charlie had years of experience as a mechanic and Tom thought he had the stuff to work for him. After all, one did have to endure a lot to work for Tom, including the proverbial *let it slip off your shoulders* routine.

Eugenia Simpkins, who lived directly across the street, peeked out her front window. She noticed that Mrs. Foster seemed a little harried and then she saw why; two boys appeared at first and then a girl. "Three of them. Time to bake cookies," she said to no one in particular.

Just then something caught her eye, something she was totally unprepared for. This time she took a closer look at the little girl. How had she missed it? The nose and the shape of the head, this little *dumpling* as she dubbed her at that exact moment, had Down syndrome. She judged her to be about eight or nine years old. She found people with Down syndrome to be highly intelligent and able to use more of their intellect than most people. They just couldn't express themselves as others did and therefore were labeled unkindly. "So sad," she muttered to herself.

Differently Double

Chapter Four

It was early evening and Lydia, along with her parents, Matt and Karen Bell, Karen's mother, Eugenia Simpkins and Matt's father, Dave, were eating dinner. The conversation at the dinner table was light, teasing and lively. Dave, Lydia's grandfather, was an FBI profiler and he would be leaving on a new assignment very soon.

"I'm still not old enough to retire, so I'll go where they send me until I get *over the hill*," he said lightly.

"You should join the force here," said his son Matt, a local policeman.

Lydia, her mouth full of food, nodded her head and swallowing her food shouted "yes!"

"I'll think about that. Sounds like a doable idea," said Dave, smiling.

"Just don't retire in twenty years or I'll be too old to enjoy your company," said Eugenia.

They all laughed.

"Did you meet the new people across the street from me?" inquired Eugenia. She was biting into her last mouthful of lemon meringue pie.

"I think one of the boys is your age," she said looking at Lydia. "Looks like a nice family. The little girl has Down syndrome. She's a real cutie and very, very strong-headed from what I've seen."

"They usually are," remarked Karen.

Eugenia continued, "I'm baking some cookies for them, but I want them to get settled in before I bring them over."

Differently Double

Chapter Five

Her pink slacks, turquoise sneakers and matching pink tee shirt with sparkles was a perfect outfit to explore in. Her hair was fashioned in two pigtails, both sticking straight out from just behind her ears. Little Mandy Foster smelled the horses, and sometimes heard them whinny or snort. She now had the opportunity to see where those noises and smells came from, so she made her way to Dottie's horse paddock across the dirt road from her home. Dottie lived next door to Eugenia and both women were the best of friends.

In the middle of the paddock stood Ferd, a twenty-five-year-old chestnut gelding. He was sleeping, but his ears twitched as he sensed someone near. He opened one eye and noticed the small figure making its way into the paddock with him. He watched as the little girl moved toward him and then she sat down in front of him. He opened both his eyes. She was staring up into them. Her eyes were wide and smiling and she started to talk to him. Her words would make no sense to any human, but Ferd understood her and was respectful and listened.

He extended his velvet muzzle toward her. She giggled and clumsily patted his cheek. His upper lip quivered as he tried to nuzzle her.

He blew out hot breath from his nostrils and she giggled again and got up. Ferd took two steps toward her then turned and headed for his favorite spot: the sand pit. His sand pit. Now, deep in the sandy area of the paddock, Ferd got down on his front knees and the rest of him followed. Flopping on his side he began to roll. Mandy came over into the sand pit and laid down on her back and did the same thing. He let out a squeal and she laughed.

In the house, not far from the barn, Dottie and Eugenia were having their morning cup of tea. Dottie put her arm on Eugenia's and asked, "what's that noise?"

Hearing a small laugh, Dottie bolted off the chair and raced through the back door with Eugenia close behind.

They were not prepared to see what they saw; horse and little girl having a sand bath together.

Dot let out a laugh while Eugenia, out of breath, joined her at the paddock fence.

"Ol' Ferd has a new friend," said Eugenia.

Running feet behind them caused both women to turn and see a very terrified mother bounding up the driveway toward them. "Oh my God," she screeched.

"Not a good idea to spook a horse in an unpleasant situation," said Dottie, firmly. "Besides Ferd is not one I'd approach if I were a stranger."

Eugenia had her finger to her mouth in the silence gesture. "They know where their feet are. Not the same for some of us," she whispered, conspiratorially.

Dottie called to Ferd, who lifted his head. "Get over here you big terd."

Mandy giggled at this and said, "terd, terd"

Her mother rolled her eyes.

Dottie started laughing and so did the little girl's mother as Eugenia shouted, "Ferd the Terd."

As they both stood, Ferd shook his head and nuzzled the little girl who was covered in sand. She shook her head and her pigtails projected sand in all directions. Ferd neighed, backed up a step and looked at her with his head cocked to one side. The little girl started walking toward the fence, all the while in constant conversation with the horse. Ferd followed closely, occasionally shaking or bending his head as if he understood every word she said.

Dottie smiled and said, "My God, she seems to be able to talk to him, like she knows horse. That's a language I've failed miserably at for the last twenty years."

"She could have been killed," stammered the mother.

"I don't think so," said Dottie. "Ferd is a big pain in the ass most times, but he does have his soft side."

Somehow Ferd knew that the little girl belonged to the distraught lady. He herded Mandy toward her and when she climbed over the bottom bar of the fence, he assisted her efforts by giving her a nudge.

"Well," said Dottie, hands on her hips, "I wish you were this helpful when I try to put a saddle on you, you big, dumb goofball."

The horse looked at her as if understanding every word she said and gave her his biggest laugh, showing both his top and bottom teeth.

"I'm Ginger," said the mom. "This is Mandy."

"I'm Dot and this is Eugenia. We're your across-the-street neighbors."

Ginger nodded to both women. "Mandy has Down syndrome and is enrolled in the school down the road."

"Yes, they come here a few times a year to show the kids the horses. It's good for them to be out and about," said Dottie.

Ginger, Eugenia and Dottie exchanged small talk while Mandy scooped up rocks in her hand and placed them on small piles. Ferd stood watching her and occasionally snorted his approval. She would smile up at him and laugh.

Ginger told the women that she had a master's degree in history from the State University at Albany. When Mandy was born, both her and her husband decided that she should be a stay-at-home mom and care for the children. This she gladly did, but she volunteered some of her time at the Down's Center in Albany, doing outreach work. When her husband accepted the position of mechanic at the junkyard, both thought it would be a welcome change from the large public schools of the city area.

This information planted a seed in both Eugenia and Dottie's heads that maybe, just maybe, Ginger would be interested in taking over the historian position vacated when the town historian died the previous year. They decided to ask Claire, the local librarian, if she thought it would be a good idea. After all, Claire would have to share a space with her in the library building if she accepted.

Ginger smiled and said, "I'm not used to a close-knit community like this one. Everyone knows everybody and I know I'll do fine and all, but I do worry."

"About what?" said Dottie.

"Oh, how we'll fit in is all."

"Nothing to worry about, really. If you're worried about Mandy here, I'm sure she'll be fine. The folks here may seem gruff for most parts, but we all have large hearts," said Eugenia.

"We have lots of organizations and for lack of entertainment you can always join our psycho group," Dottie snickered.

"Psycho group?" asked Ginger.

"We have a paranormal group that meets monthly. We discuss all matters concerning the metaphysical and new ideas in psychic research."

"My daughter is a Reiki master," said Eugenia, quietly.

"Oh," said Ginger, "I'm Reiki second degree. I want to get my Reiki master, but time and money are a problem right now. I got it to help me and my daughter cope. It has helped. I would love to meet your daughter."

Then Ginger sighed and eyeing the two women warily, she said, "I think my house is haunted."

Both women shook their heads knowingly.

"Yeah, I do believe that. There was a suicide in there many years ago. It does need a good cleansing. Father Munro will be able to help you. He's the man to do the job," said Dottie.

"Father Munro?" asked Ginger.

"He works with ghosts and spirits. Great man and funny too. Give him a call or better yet, visit him. He lives over on the back street next to the Catholic church. He's the priest."

~

Over the ensuing weeks, Father Munro, the local Catholic Priest, was called in to perform a house blessing for the family. After the blessing, the house finally quieted down from its past abuse and became a comfortable and happy home.

Differently Double

Chapter Six

It didn't take long to get the word out, and on Wednesday night at four-thirty the drive in front of the office of Pederson's junkyard was filled with kids of varying ages, all carrying books. Josh came running when he heard Tom bellow "what the hell? Is this an invasion of some sort?"

Josh started laughing, "No, just a study group," he told Tom.

"A what?" shrieked Tom.

"We're trying to get Alex up to speed. His first exam with Ol' Battleaxe is Friday and we're trying to get him out of ninth grade and into twelfth."

"Holy hell," said Tom, shaking his head from side to side. "What next?"

A wheeler rolled into the side yard with Alex on board. He took off his helmet and goggles and just stared at the assemblage.

He knew some of the kids, but there were a lot more he didn't know. They ranged in ages from twelve to sixteen. Some were girls. One in particular, Alex found out later, was named Christine. She was particularly snooty but according to Kenny Gaw, another good friend of his, she was a genius. With a little bribing, she was encouraged to help out.

"Ok, ok listen up," shouted Josh. "Sit on the grass, on the picnic tables and as soon as the *vic*, I mean Alex, is off work here in about ten minutes we'll start."

Alex just stared. He had not seen so many kids in his life and he felt overwhelmed and very self-conscious. Lydia and Olivia came into the yard with their friend, Louis, followed by Louis's little sister and his mother.

Tom just stared. "Mean-looking bunch, best behave myself," he muttered as he disappeared into the office and shut the door.

"Ok, Christine, you fire off the questions and we'll let Alex here have a crack at it. Let's start with American history eighth grade. Remember we have to put Ol 'Battleaxe in her place," shouted Josh. They all nodded. All the kids had been carefully selected and told of the circumstances before coming this afternoon.

They all knew that maybe this kid held the secret to unlocking their losing streak at basketball for the last twelve seasons and they were willing to help out in any way they could.

"Alex, this is your study group. Group, this is Alex," said Josh.

Just then a motorcycle shot into the yard. Two boys got off and removed their helmets.

"So, this is the hot shot ball player," said one of the boys.

"Knock it off," said Josh. Both boys were his teammates.

Alex went over to the motorcycle and said, "Nice Harley, a 1985 low rider. You know they're bringing 'em back now. They were and still are very popular. Looks like it had some work done on it. Not original paint but very nice. That's an 80 Ci engine. Looks like the original."

The larger of the two boys had a sneer on his face, but it was disappearing rapidly.

He said, "Yeah, thanks, it skips some."

Alex nodded his head in agreement and said "I bet whoever worked on it last put the wrong wires on. I bet you have plugs that don't ma- ma- match either."

Both boys looked at him in awe.

"I'm restoring a 1994 VR1000. Came in from a crash. Dream is to get it up and running again," Alex muttered.

"Wow," said the second of the two boys, "a Harley VR 1000? Original!"

Tom came out at the sound of the bike coming into the yard. He looked it over. "Needs some work in tune up," he said, "but it sounds real nice, just like a Harley should."

Both boys looked at him bewildered.

"That's my dad," said Alex.

"Enough, we're here to get this man into twelfth grade, not motorcycle one-o-one," shouted Josh impatiently.

"Hi, Mr. Pederson," said a voice from the crowd. It came from Louis's sister. She held her mother's hand tightly and smiled up at him.

Tom nodded and gave her a bewildered smile.

"Alright, question number one," said Christine and on and on came the questions. Alex fired the answers right back at her without hesitation.

"Give me some hard ones, will ya," he said laughing.

"Alright, we're changing books. You're getting homework tonight, hear me?" she shrilled. "You're getting English literature."

"What period?" asked Alex.

"Ooohhhhh good grief," she said, slapping her forehead.

Then Christine spun around and faced Josh. "You didn't tell me all, Joshie boy," she said, irritably.

Josh just looked from her to Alex. Alex shrugged his shoulders and winced.

Christine spun around and faced Alex. She was now ready for war. "Ok, what Irish author wrote a satire on the treatment of the poor and what was the title of the book?"

"Swift," said Alex. "Yes, Swift. Really got the English going on social reform. *Gulliver's Travels*. I personally didn't like the book, but."

"Ok, that does it, you're writing an essay."

"I don't write," said Alex, purely distressed.

"Well you better start," she sneered. "I'll pick it up tomorrow before noon."

"Demanding bitch," said Tom who was standing nearby. His comment was low enough so only Josh heard him. Josh glanced at him sideways and snickered.

Olivia rolled her eyes. Olivia and Christine did not get along. Christine was several grades ahead of Olivia and thought she knew everything. Knowing everything was Olivia's territory.

Just then the tall figure of a woman approached. She had hidden herself near the gate but out of sight. She had been there listening for at least thirty minutes. The crowd of youngsters intrigued her so she had to find out what they were doing. She was carrying two bags of groceries and she had sat them down along the chain link fence. As she straightened out, she noticed the box in the fence next to the mailbox and she smiled. "What kids had to go through to learn," she thought "and yet others who had all the learning available don't even use the resources."

When she heard herself referred to as Ol' Battleaxe, she smiled sadly. She knew all these kids and when kids were among kids, she could imagine what some of the other teachers were referred to. She had heard Mr. Benson called Worm and Mrs. Grady called Mole. She had to smile, it was funny and let's face it, she did the same thing growing up.

There was a hushed silence as she approached.

"Oh, hi, Miss Goodwin," said Christine in her most charming, syrupy voice.

"Continue," Miss Goodwin said, a broad smile on her face. "From what I have heard Alex has already passed the ninth grade, but math scores will tell. And let's face it, the Ol' Battleaxe is a fair person."

Several faces in the crowd turned a shade of pink and there were many glances downward.

"I haven't had too much math," muttered Alex. "I understand numbers and all."

"That's ok," said Kenny and Christine in unison. "We'll get you ready."

Amy Goodwin raised her eyebrows. "This is going to be interesting," she thought.

~

Every afternoon Kenny, Christine and several others tutored Alex. They had him doing algebra and he had a good grasp of trigonometry and polynomials. Alex thought polynomials were really fun. Christine could not, for the life of her, imagine that anyone in their right mind would think polynomials were fun.

By Friday Alex was ready for eleventh grade, with the exception of English composition. That was his real challenge.

"You're a good writer, but you can't write the way your father talks or for that matter the way others you know talk. The f word is off bounds, do you hear me?" said Amy, sternly. "There are other ways to shock than the f bomb."

Alex nodded.

Chapter Seven

Gene removed his baseball cap, a requirement if you wanted to get served at the café on Main Street. He placed it on one of the pegs of the oversize hat rack installed near the front door. His dark brown hair was cut in military style and his hazel eyes took in the clientele who were eating and talking. Gene smiled and nodded to several of the clientele and sat down at the counter.

"Usual Gene?" asked Suzie, one of the owners of the establishment.

"Yes," he said in his soft, southern accent and smiled at her.

Gene was a well-liked guy and a regular at the café. He was quiet, had good, sound advice when asked and a gentleness that was uncanny. He was a favorite among the groups that frequented here. Gene rode an old bicycle and boarded at Mrs. Henshaw's, just up the street from the Catholic Church. He helped her with her antique business. He made her deliveries for her, kept the lawn mowed and worked in the antique shop most days. He did a lot of the buying. More and more customers came into the store now that Gene was managing it and the shop had regular hours.

Mrs. Henshaw was not accustomed to regular hours and didn't like opening if there was something else going on in town, especially something she could gossip about. Gene liked the *Ol' Gal* as he called her and he kept his small apartment off the back of the building clean and the shop as well.

Gene didn't know why he was urged to come here to upstate New York. What was it with the voices in his head that told him he needed to be *here?* Why? He had never stepped foot in the state in his life nor ever needed or intended to; until now.

In the light of a sultry afternoon, he headed back to the shop to finish fixing a lamp that had been dropped off by a customer. He stood on the porch of the shop and surveyed the landscape. Mrs. Henshaw's small house was across the driveway from the large barn filled with antiques. Attached to the barn was a small building that served as his apartment.

From here he could see the steeple of the Catholic Church, the back sides of the buildings along Main Street and the supermarket. To the rear of the shop were hay fields and the woods with a path through them to the lake at the Fish and Game Club.

Gene's early childhood experiences were nice enough with his mother, grandma and grandpa. They were hard scrabble, dirt poor Alabama farmers. When his family all passed on, he had enlisted in the navy, served for three enlistments and got out.

"Why here?" he mused as he made his way into the interior of the dimly lit shop. He knew he had the opportunity to buy the business from the old lady and pursue his dream of owning an antiques shop. And maybe, just maybe, dabble in a few of his favorite hobbies, like fishing, reading, tinkering with old stuff and the paranormal and pseudo-sciences. He had managed to get involved with several organizations in town like the Fish and Game Club and the Chamber of Commerce, but there was one group he dearly wanted to be a part of and that was the psychic and paranormal group run by Eugenia Simpkins and several of her friends.

Chapter Eight

Dave and his son Matt were quietly having coffee in the kitchen of Matt's home. Lydia's cat, Spyder, rubbed Dave's legs, purring and attempting to get onto his lap. Dave had his chair pulled all the way into the table, preventing her from doing so.

"She's a pain sometimes, but she really likes you," Matt told his father. "If you back away from this table, she'll jump."

Dave nodded and smiled.

"She's not allowed on the table or the counter. Off limits. Put my foot down when we got her." Matt said. "But, she's gettin old."

"Anyway, this particular job came up yesterday," Dave continued. "Double homicide in Alabama, years ago. Seems that some people bought this property way back in the woods. They found two bodies in the barn, wrapped up and put in barrels. If that wasn't bad enough, the new owners were getting ready to renovate the house and put in a swimming pool and they uncovered some bones. Some of them animal and some human. The police are investigating who lived there all those years ago and how long the bones have been in the ground. So, my boss wants me to go and have a look."

"Where in Alabama?" asked Matt.

"Tomisina," said Dave.

Matt nodded.

"After you left, Mom sold the house and moved in with a guy called Bradley. Don't remember his last name. We moved to Tomisina," said Matt, thoughtfully.

Dave nodded and said, "Yes, I remember. Remember, I kept an eye on you although I wasn't able to go anywhere near you or her. I remember the mailing address as a PO Box in Tomisina."

"God-for-saken, out-of-the-way place. Weeds, trees and bugs everywhere. Lots of places for crawfish and some good fishin holes though. The house was old and there was a small barn and some outbuilding of some sort," remarked Matt.

"Something bothering you?" inquired Dave.

Karen, walking into the kitchen, looked quizzically at her husband.

"Just a niggling feeling, bordering on... scary, that's all," said Matt as he sighed and smiled up at his wife.

"I hear ya," said Dave. "I remember a great place where they used to sell the best pulled pork on the continent. This big fellow with the mom who ran the place. He did all the butchering."

"Yeah, that place near the Shell Oil refinery," said Matt, chuckling. "He also had the best crawfish on Friday. He went all night on Thursday, his day off, and caught craws. People lined up for miles just to get a couple pounds. He had a hell of a personality."

Both men smiled, thinking of fond memories of pulled pork and the jovial personality of the large black man with the big heart.

~

Lydia was walking home, on this the last week of summer vacation when she noticed a familiar car in the driveway and she raced the last one-hundred yards to the house. As her foot landed on the first step, Dave was exiting the back door.

"Hi Gramps," she shouted. "Dad here?"

He hugged her and nodded to the kitchen. Her father sat at the kitchen table while her mother, seeing the exchange with her grandfather, got up to get her a glass of iced tea from the refrigerator.

Chapter Nine

Coming down off the porch steps Dave stopped to notice a man riding a bicycle. He hadn't seen a bike that old in a long time. "From the sixties," he mused although that style was coming back into popularity again. "New is just a reflection of the old," he thought.

Dave started walking to his apartment. When he had finished his last case, he had approached Larry, a medical examiner and local coroner, and asked about the apartment he had for rent. Larry and his partner, Steve, lived in a large, old Victorian on the Main Street, not far from where Lydia, Matt and Karen lived. It was the family home Larry had inherited from his family. The house had a wrap-around front porch and a long driveway at the side of the house. Parking was at the back in front of an old carriage house where Dave now comfortably ensconced himself. The carriage house was painted red to match the main house with white gingerbread trim and a front door painted turquoise. Often Dave would sit on the front porch of the large house with a beer and converse with both men about all sorts of things.

Steve was an anthropologist with the state. He groomed himself meticulously and kept his ebony skin smooth and this belied his fifty-seven years of existence. He was funny, fun to be around and had a dry sense of humor bordering on the ridiculous at times. He was interested in all things folklore and followed the pseudo-sciences like an obsession. Anything to do with lay lines, time warps and inter-stellar travel Steve was fluent on. The high school kids adored him and he was thought of as a genius and a mentor, especially when he got on one of his fiery tangents.

Steve's penchant for anything pink and Larry's sarcastic demeanor were a good combination, but Dave didn't fare so well the night Larry had to work and Steve convinced Dave to go to a used car auction in Syracuse, an hour-and-a-half away.

When they came home with the old, pink Cadillac, which Steve promptly named Matilda, after a long-deceased aunt, Dave though he would be homeless within minutes of parking it in the driveway.

Larry, spying the car, just stood there, glaring at it. It took all of two minutes for the stream to come out of his ears and the explosion to begin. Larry's face was a vivid shade of puce when he shouted, "What prompted you to buy this...this..."

"Vintage Cadillac?" Steve interjected with a sweet, approving smile on his face.

Larry stomped up the porch, slammed the door and it was two weeks before Larry spoke to Dave again.

Dave admired the two men, especially Steve, but he did have questions about their lifestyle. So, on this late August evening Dave sat on the front porch in an oversize white wicker chair, nursing a beer and nibbling on pretzels, wheat crackers and local goat cheese. He had finally amassed enough courage to ask his friend and landlord what it was like to be gay.

Steve, sitting in an identical white wicker chair, laughed and became contemplative.

"I mean," said Dave, "I really don't give a rat's ass about your sexual orientation, I would just like to know more about it. Just curious, and of course, I listen to the girls," meaning Dottie and Eugenia and their paranormal group.

"Well, that explains a lot," said Steve, chuckling. "I mean the metaphysical thing and our past lives and all does make some sense. But feelings are feelings and if we chance to meet in this life again, well, we start where we left off, I guess. Regardless of our sex. Good enough explanation as most I've heard."

Dottie and Eugenia, along with Steve and several others in town, had formed a metaphysical group. It was popular and consisted of professionals and non-professionals alike, regardless of beliefs. Christians, Wicans, several agnostics and the local Catholic Priest, who was an honorary member, met monthly and rotated venues. Discussions were lively and topics included the latest research into the paranormal, psychiatry and psychology, dowsing, and the healing modalities such as Reiki, Healing Touch, and Angel Healing or IET.

"I just don't want to be hypnotized and brought back to past lives. What if they dig up something I can't handle? Like I was Marilyn Monroe in my past life, or Tallulah Bankhead or some silly female like Boopsy LaDue or Betty Boop? My God I would really be traumatized," said Steve, looking rather perplexed.

"Steve. I really don't think there's anything you can't handle. You're a real bear," said Dave.

"I have soft spots I cover with enthusiasm and cynicism," said Steve, contritely.

"Don't we all," said Dave, smiling.

"Well, getting back to your question," Steve sighed a deep sigh, "It's the friendship thing. It's a relationship."

He continued, "We're human, that's all. Actually, divine beings having a human experience. Nothing else matters, not hair, skin color, sexual orientation or religious beliefs. Nothing, but how we interact with others having this same human experience," said Steve, reflectively. "Incidentally, thank you for being my friend. I don't think I've ever said that to you."

He looked directly at Dave, who looked a little embarrassed.

Steve continued, "This place. Being here has changed my life. This is the kind of town that we all dream of. It's got to be the water or something, but we all do get along. Sure, we agree to disagree, but generally there are no real snobs here. I know the local evangelical Christians would like to take me to task, but the mainline Christians are ok with us. I mean, I have some gay friends that are more extreme than some of the far right Christians. Whatever floats your boat. You don't have to be my best friend, just give me some slack and respect me as a fellow traveler. That's all I ask and I'll give you the same"

Steve looked directly at Dave, who had a thoughtful, questioning look on his face. Steve smiled a knowing smile, nodded his head a few times and said, "ahhh the sex thing."

Dave, looking relieved when he said this, smiled thoughtfully and nodded his head.

"Sex is an expression of ultimate love. Yes, it has its reproduction thing attached and all the other stuff society wants to pin onto it, but the true consummation of the love act has always been for the shared bliss. Notice I say shared and bliss. It's not rape, nor guilt, nor abuse, nor kinky acts of pleasure where all you have is bang boom and it's over. And, it is not for sale. No, none of that crap. It is a shared knowing of another's soul, more or less. Kids come along sometimes, but I think God created the sex act just for the right to get really close to him through and with another human being."

[27]

Dave nodded thoughtfully as Steve continued.

"Well, it's just like any other relationship that involves love. Respect for the other person, especially. I really can't explain it, but it just happens. You're partners, lovers, friends, all the quality things that make up a good relationship with two consenting people. A relationship, if you want to put it that way, regardless of the sex of the partner."

"I remember when I was living near Nayak," said Dave, thoughtfully, "near the city. I had two neighbors. Both women, both married to the other. One was built like a trucker with short, cropped hair and she was real obnoxious and cynical. The other was a real knockout. Feminine, cute, obviously in love with her partner. I would marvel at their relationship and of course they would have disagreements, but not a lot of them. It was an easy understanding between them both."

"So, the trucker one reminded you of *Adamas' Jerk* only with a vagina," said Steve, with some brevity in his voice.

Dave laughed until tears came to his eyes and shook his head yes. "I guess there is really no difference," said Dave, reflecting on the image in his mind.

"No, there isn't. The whole thing is to be comfortable in your own skin. Those who are trite, judgmental and blow with the wind, they're the ones who will never be happy with who they truly are and with who others are. They are scared to really get to know themselves because they're scared at what they might find. How will we change when we find out stuff about us and we face our truth, our fears instead of hiding under a façade for the rest of our lives? I think that could give one a whole new meaning on life. So, accept who you are and go on. Change if you have to, but embrace who you are; your distinctness, your selfness... here I go getting on my soap box again. Not good," mused Steve.

~

There was a snuffling sound and then grunts as a very overweight bulldog attempted to climb up the steps and onto the porch. The dog was brindle and white and as large around as he was tall... "Come on Howie," said Steve, "you can do it."

The dog finally made it to the top and rolled over to catch his breath. When he rolled over, the dog reminded Dave of roadkill; dead for a day and bloated in the sun.

Now Howie was stuck. No matter how hard he tried to upright himself, he was stuck, like a turtle on its back, four legs waving frantically in the air.

"Oh, for Christ's sake," said Steve reaching over to right the dog. Steve patted his head as Howie looked gratefully at him, his large, lolling tongue hanging out of his mouth.

"Reminds me of a beach ball," said Dave thoughtfully.

"One of these days he's going to beach and no one will be around to rescue him. It's Larry and the beef jerky he feeds him."

Steve's brow furrowed as he continued. "He's really the only thing that connects Larry to his past. He was married to Katherine DeSilva and this little, overweight guy was her dog. I think it's the only thing Larry got out of the divorce settlement. That, and getting out of the city and back here to his boyhood home."

Dave furrowed his brows, "Katherine DeSilva, the opera singer?" said Dave incredulously.

"One and the same," said Steve. "Don't ask," waving his long-fingered hand in Dave's direction. "It's a long story and they're still friends and all, it's just that Larry found himself and that was that."

Chapter Ten

Dave would be in Mobile, Alabama by late afternoon. In Mobile, he met with local police and they showed him the skeletal remains of several of the bodies that had been taken to the morgue.

"Tomorrow, we'll show you the crime scene," said his boss, Brian Nedo, who had flown in from DC to join the team. Nedo had greeted him with "I guess you're part of the team this time, just please, no mention of ghosts and paranormal," alluding to the last case he was on with Dave.

Dave just smiled and nodded.

It was early the next morning and the heat was sweltering. "We'll pick up the police captain in Shelbyville and go from there," said Nedo. "He says we'll need a bulldozer to get into the place. It's all overgrown and, of course, with the attempted construction, it's a real mess. You familiar with this area?"

"Yeah, raised here. Married here. Had two kids here, then it all went south in a hurry," said Dave.

Nedo nodded and said, "so you know the area?"

"Yeah. Later I'll show you where some of the best pulled pork comes from if he's still here."

"I'm for that," said Nedo, excitement in his voice as he anticipated a fantastic gastric event. "My favorite."

They pulled onto a dirt road and rode for several miles. They could see the crime scene tape wrapped around trees before they stopped at the side of the road and got out of the vehicles.

"We'll walk from here," said one of the officers.

"Where in hell are we?" said Nedo.

"Well," drawled one officer, "go left and you're into the Shell Oil refinery. Straight back you're into the bayou."

"Anyone else live on this road?" Nedo questioned.

"Up about three miles just before you get out onto the main road again is a nice new house. That's all."

Nedo nodded.

They began walking down the overgrown, weedy path swathed in kudzu, copperleaf, ferns and vetches and soon came upon a tiny house. At one time, this could have been a cute house, but time and the elements had taken its toll. The door was half off of its hinges and it was obvious that animals had made their home here for many years.

Something niggled at Dave's brain. His memory insisted he had been here before, but how and why?

Mummified food sat in a refrigerator, long past the state of decay. The pantry was still filled with various canned goods along with mason jars filled with tomatoes and kale.

The bed in the first floor bedroom showed rumpled sheets and stains on the covers on the bed. Several small brown spots lay on the floor. The crime lab had been called in and activity at the house was like a swarm of bees.

Dave tested the stairs and climbed to the second floor. Only two bedrooms off to one corner of the house and they were both small. A tiny corner closet held the remains of towels and linens, a mop and a broom. The windows were broken and glass and leaves littered the floor and the beds. They were still made up and looked quaint; sad and forlorn. Something was taking him back, back into a time he wanted to forget.

He slid a bureau drawer open. A few pieces of boys underwear, socks, several tees and a pair of shorts. He rifled through them, looking for what? He didn't know, just something. "Who were these people?" he thought.

He looked under the old linoleum that lined the drawers, it came up with tears, but he persisted. Nothing.

Several dead crawfish and fishing lures and hooks lined the bottom drawer. He looked under one bed and riffled through the bed covers remembering his own youth where treasures were kept hidden under the mattress. He lifted one edge of the mattress. Sure enough, a small piece of paper fluttered out. It was faded, the pencil lines barely legible on the lined notebook paper. It was shaped in the form of a heart. Like a valentine from a child that couldn't afford a store bought one. *I love my brother* is all it said.

Dave smiled sadly. "Evidence," he muttered.

He looked around the room one last time and went to the other room. It was larger. He began rifling through the drawers. He found the usual clothing of another boy, this one was very thin and tall. The boy in the first room had been a little heavier and shorter. In the third drawer he found a small pile of rocks of various shapes and sizes. Good rocks for throwing he mused. He noticed that some of the rocks were covered with a coating of something. It was brown in color and the hue looked like what was spattered on the floor downstairs. He carefully put them back but didn't close the drawer.

He looked in the usual places under the bed and when he pulled up the mattress and found something that chilled him to the bone. The faded, pink dress of a small child lay neatly folded under the mattress in the middle of the bed. He carefully unfolded the garment and again those brown stains were evident around the collar and down the back of the dress on one side. He laid the garment onto the bed and called to Nedo. "Got something up here. Need the lab," he shouted.

Nedo was the first up the stairs. Dave nodded at the bed and backed away.

"Found some pictures in the silverware drawer in the kitchen that's all," said Nedo. "Funny, they were under the drawer organizer. Just family pics. Looks like from the seventies or so. Got the gals going through records on who owned the place in the sixties through the nineties. Today all this land is owned by the oil refinery. They don't like too many people living near the plant, so they buy up everything in sight."

"Got a lot of work to do here," said a young lab tech as he walked into the room. "I'll get more evidence bags. Won't know what the splatter is for sure until tomorrow, but we have a good assumption."

Nedo nodded and called the office. When he was done he asked one of the officers, "anything on the owners of this dump?"

"History of the place goes back a long ways. The local historian, man in his eighties, knows the people round here. Lives right in Port Prince, just down the road a ways."

"Let's go," said Nedo. "This place gives me the creeps."

It was hot and dusty and the salty smell of the bayou assailed their nostrils as they drove toward their destination.

"A lot of this was destroyed with Katrina," said Dave. "FEMA did these folks no favors and they're still paying for it. Lot of them have nothing after that storm."

"Should have wiped out the whole place," said Nedo, observing the dilapidated and abandoned houses.

They knocked on the door of a light brick ranch. A tall woman answered the door and Nedo introduced himself.

"He's in the back room, coolin' off. Go on through. Sweet tea?" she asked. Nedo and Dave both nodded their heads yes.

"Hello, Mr. Burnside," said Nedo, "we're from the FBI."

"Expectin ya," is all the old man said. "Sit down, take a load off." He motioned to two overstuffed chairs.

The tall, slender woman handed them each a frosty glass of iced tea and sat on the arm of the couch near her husband.

"You've been around here a long time," said Dave, "and we need some help. Over on the dirt road, just before you get onto the main road for the plant..."

"Ahh yes, the old Sellers Place," interjected Burnside. "Lot of police activity there, so my son-in-law says. He's a police officer. Works downtown. Said bodies recovered there. Now Sellers, was a good guy as I recall. Owned a cat fishing business down on the Pilcan Cove there. Had a boat, but then he got that no good son of his involved and it all went to hell. Some people are just born plain mean and that kid sure was. He was abusive and mean. Some say he killed his first wife. That thar woman he brought round last time, she was nice but a little coarse. Ya know, gave ya the impression that she knew men all too well. Never saw her drunk, but boy could she swear. She could knock the skin off a pole cat with some-those words come out of her mouth. Had this little bitty girl and a nice boy with her. It was back in the eighties maybe. The old folks were long gone before that. They were the ones who built the place. Of course, the bayou came up near the back of the barn, but after the last one, the storm I mean, that all changed. It's a wonder the place didn't go down in all the wind, but it's well protected with all the trees and folks around here say it's haunted."

Dave felt nauseated, like he was being punched in the stomach. "Excuse me," he said abruptly and left the room. He headed for the outside and for the tree near the car. He started to cry. He shook violently as he sank to the ground at the base of a large, old pecan tree.

The woman, obviously shaken by his behavior, ran after him. She stood over him, an anxious look on her face.

"Please, I have to know something," Dave said hoarsely.

She leaned against the car, still looking at him with concern. Her husband joined her with Nedo at his side. The old man carefully laid his cane down on the grass and sat down next to Dave.

"Well young fella, you look like hell," he said.

Ignoring the comment, Dave plowed on. "What happened to the little girl?"

The woman looked thoughtfully at Dave and said, "no one knows. She was there for, I'd say six months or a year and then she disappeared. They looked all over the bayou. They had a search party out for her, but in the end, nothing. Most people surmise that a gator got hold of her, but there were other rumors too," said Mrs. Burnside.

"Like what?" said Dave gruffly.

"Well, the older boy, I'd say he was maybe sixteen, he was a mean son-of-a-bitch just like his father. A lot of folks round here would hire him out for odd jobs. He never cared about school. The younger boy, well one day he wasn't there. A few years later and they're all gone. Poof. Gone," she said.

Nedo just stared at Dave, who was still sitting.

Dave said quietly, "The girl was Selma, the younger boy was Matt. They were my kids. The older boy was…"

"Garrett," said Mrs. Burnside, almost shouting. "Garrett. I went to school with his father Bradley. Now Bradley, there was a piece of work like my husband says. His mother insisted we call him Bradley, not Brad just Bradley. He was sly and very manipulating and really creepy and grew up to be a real wise guy who said he would someday own his father's catfish business."

It grew silent and the chirring of locusts broke the quiet of the late afternoon air.

"I loved that little girl," said Mrs. Burnside reflectively. "She was so full of life and so full of questions. She wanted to know everything. She ran around all the time, no supervision at all, just wild and free. The younger boy as well. Then life takes over."

"Yup, life takes over," said Dave, struggling to his feet. He gave Mr.

Burnside a hands up and held onto him.

"Son, come on in and sit, please. It'll do you good," he said, quietly.

Dave nodded his head and headed for the porch and a chair.

"Here's your tea or you want somethin' stronger?" asked Mrs. Burnside.

Nedo couldn't imagine how Dave felt. If that was his own child, then what? What would he do?

"I'm sorry, Dave," he said, lost for words.

"I had to find out; that's why I took this assignment. I had a feeling and so did Matt."

An hour later Dave looked composed enough and the two men left the Burnsides.

"I'll drive," said Nedo. "Feel like eating?" he asked hesitantly.

"Yes," said Dave. "I wanna go to the Pelican and have raw oysters, gumbo and a beer. Just down the road a ways. Past the plant, take a right and it's on the left. Eating seems to calm me. Take my mind off things."

Nedo grinned and said, "sounds like a plan ol' buddy."

Dave smiled sadly as he said, "we'll talk over gumbo and oysters."

"We took several pics into evidence," said Nedo quietly.

"I'd like to see them," said Dave, in a hushed and resigned tone.

"Over what in hell did you say and oysters?" asked Nedo.

Dave laughed, "gumbo, Brian, gumbo."

"I'm game" said Nedo.

They parked in the parking lot of the large restaurant and marina. Boats were coming and going, mostly fishing trawlers. Music and laughter emanated from the restaurant. Even the outside deck was busy.

"Inside or out?" said a middle-aged waitress who wore a black dress and a white apron.

"Near the window on the side facing the river," said Dave.

She nodded her head, "Been here before?"

Dave nodded yes and they followed her.

"Nice place," remarked Nedo as they walked toward their table.

"It's nice. Good atmosphere," said Dave. "We can go south tomorrow or when we get a chance. Then we'll go to the fish camp. Yup, Felix's at sunset, what a view."

The gumbo came and the beer followed by raw oysters.

"I hate to spoil the meal," Nedo said cautiously just before coffee and pecan pie arrived.

"I want to see the pics; I have to," said Dave.

Nedo cautiously slid the small packet with half a dozen pictures toward him. The first one was of the house and the small garage. The second one pulled Dave up short. Two boys, chests bare, shorts and bare feet, taken somewhere near the front of the house. They both held fishing poles and one boy was much taller and skinnier than the second boy, who looked younger.

"Recognize the younger boy," said Dave quietly.

He pushed the picture toward Nedo who studied it thoughtfully. Nedo frowned.

Dave said quietly, "the shorter one on the left is Matt."

Nedo peered at Dave over the edge of the picture. "Oh shit," he hissed.

"Tragic story. I was not allowed anywhere near his mother, him or my daughter. When my daughter disappeared, is the last time I saw any of them until I met up with Matt last year. I'll tell you it was not good. The inquest and investigation, I mean. I was working with a unit in New York City at the time."

Dave paused, "as there was a court order against me, I made sure my son had money, or rather his mother did. At sixteen, he was told to take a hike and I made sure he was taken care of. I stayed in the background. I was with the FBI at the time and I traveled a lot, so a steady home and family was essential after the ordeal he had. He got that and to this day his foster father and mother have remained an essential part of his life. Something I'm glad for. He's a New York City cop, retired."

He looked down at another pic and this one made tears well in his eyes. Two children, one about four years, a girl and another a boy of about nine or ten stood at attention in front of a small garden.

"That's at the old house. Matt and Selma," Dave said quietly.

Not wanting to see more he placed the pictures back in the evidence envelope and pushed them toward Nedo.

"Thanks for that. I did need to see them and now...," said Dave.

"Well, it looks like we're looking for one Garrett Sellers, if he's still alive," said Nedo.

"Oh, he's still alive," said Dave. "He's still alive."

"How do you know?" asked Nedo.

"I can feel him," said Dave.

Differently Double

Chapter Eleven

His first kill. Ah yes, it was the daughter of his father's latest conquest at the time. He remembered it vividly; he was fifteen years old. She was an annoying six-year-old. She drove him to distraction until one day he just had enough and hit her on the head with a rock. She crumpled, making a funny sound deep down in her throat. Her body was limp and he panicked. He hid her first in the basement, but after a few days a funny odor was emanating from the body, so he took it to the woods and buried it deeply at the base of an old tree.

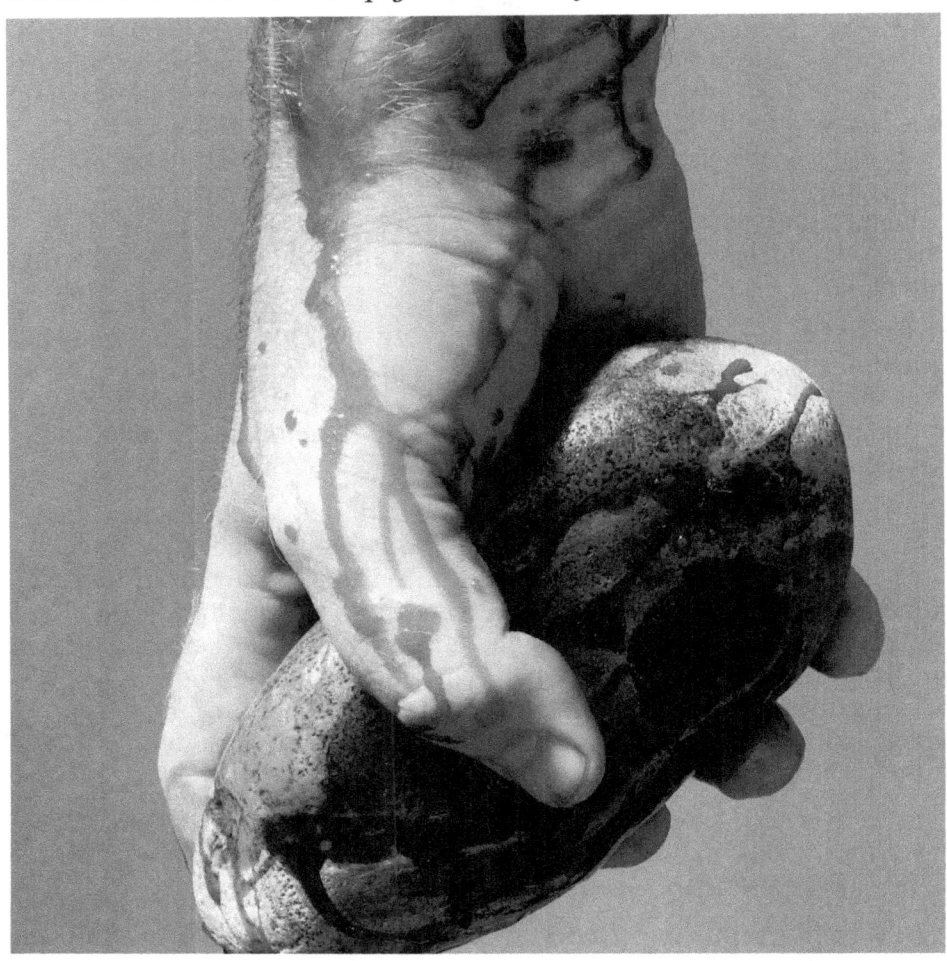

Deep down he knew her brother Matt knew what happened. Then Matt had left the fold at sixteen. His father's girlfriend just told her son to beat it and he did. But that left him, Garrett, to bear the brunt of their abusive and sadistic treatments.

That was years ago and lots of water under the bridge. He was twenty when his father finally told him to beat it. But he had taken care of them both the day he left with his weapon of choice; a rock.

~

Memories flooded Dottie. Some were so unsettling she didn't want to remember. She often thought of her sister. What ever happened to her? Dottie fled her previous life, after she had broken into a million fragile pieces...when she left Alabama. Hiding, always quick to change her appearance, she acquired a new social security card and identity and now she was here in Emeryville, New York. She was far away from Alabama and her nemesis...those memories. Always looking over her shoulder, she befriended many people and she was sure she could trust them, but...

Now, at her age, it was still hard to live with a shroud over your head all the time, constantly looking over your shoulder. Expecting the unexpected when you least expected it. She was getting better at the thinking positive thing and willing herself to remember that this was her sanctuary; hers, not the demons that possessed her.

Dottie had loved her sister and when she had to flee, it broke her heart. Her sister was caring for their mother and father, made frail and senile by hard work on a poor farm that couldn't even afford a pair of shoes for their kids. Her sister had married a man who was demanding and abusive. Dottie's brother-in-law had inherited all his father's bayou business but promptly ruined it all. They had twin boys and when her sister's divorce had occurred, thanks to Dottie's meddling and encouragement, her sister took one child and her husband took the other. The boys were five years old at the time.

Yes, Dottie remembered her brother-in-law well. She went to school with him. Privileged, abusive, always sneering... always bullying. Dottie left years after that. She fled with nothing to lose.

She was interrupted by a knock at the back door. Eugenia came into her kitchen carrying a large bouquet of roses, baby's breath and iris.

"What's this?" Eugenia chided, looking quizzically at her friend's face.

"Oh, just reminiscing," said Dottie, her brow furrowed, "on that part of my life I don't wanna reminisce about. When you get older, you tend to let a lot go and you harp on the other parts."

Eugenia sat down looking at her friend. "How long have we known each other?" she asked.

Dottie sat across from her, her gaze unbroken on her friend's face.

"I don't know if I'm ready," Dottie said quietly.

"If you don't take that first step, you'll take it to the grave. Do you want that?" Eugenia asked cautiously.

Dottie smiled sadly and said, "Hell no, I'd have to kill the bastard all over again."

Eugenia showed no surprise, but her brow furrowed and she smiled thoughtfully. "How many times have I wanted to kill someone?" she sighed.

Dottie burst out laughing. "Like Larry?" she said, referring to the coroner and Eugenia's nemesis in grade school and beyond. A little younger and a lot heavier with a penchant to push Eugenia's buttons with abandon while enjoying every minute of it, Larry still had that effect on her, many years later.

Eugenia smiled and said, "I let him push my buttons. All my fault but you know I really like him, in a sisterly sort of way. But he really pisses me off. I bet he thinks he can pee uphill in a hurricane."

Dottie glanced at Eugenia and a smile crossed her face, then she looked out the window. "After the events of the last few months, it feels good to get back on track," she mused.

Dottie looked back and straight at her friend and said, "I killed a man; at least I think I did. I snapped after he did something to my two baby girls. I killed him and then I ran. I'm still running."

Eugenia showed no surprise in her face, no sympathy either. "Your secret's safe with me. Now they'll be two of us looking over our shoulders at every little thing out of the ordinary."

"I don't know what the bastard did to my babies," said Dottie. "All I know is they were gone. Maybe he sold them, I don't think he'd have the balls to kill them, although he was mean enough. He was all about abuse and control. He thought he could control me like he did his clients and the town council and the local judges. Money talks you know. Money talks and shit walks. God, he was a despicable bastard, but when you're poor white trash and a little older than most with nowhere to go," she sighed, "it's a step up."

"More like a step up and six down," Eugenia muttered.

"I was the wild child and I took a lot of chances and I saw this as an opportunity. Should've done my homework, but when hormones are raging and time is flying, common sense goes out the window," said Dottie, sullenly.

"I was a lonely child" said Eugenia. "Decent home, nice parents and a good, supportive family. We were on the reservation until I was about ten, then we came here. Been here ever since. I was tall, dark skin, buck teeth, braids. I was treated ok, bullied a little, but I have tough skin and I could bully more. They knew enough to leave me alone. I was the star of the field hockey team, never liked basketball, but I excelled at baseball. The sports saved my ass. My husband was a kind man, quiet, a good ten years ahead of me in school. His family's all gone now."

"I had four miscarriages and then my little Karen was born. She was the light of our eyes. She was about six or seven when my husband died. Heart attack. Karen grew up following intuitively in my shoes. She has the psychic and healing gifts. Matt came along and eventually they had baby Sarah. Then the accident and Sarah died. Those were the dark days, the accident and all. Then, in answer to my prayers, Lydia comes along, although Lydia reminds me of me...a person of her own mind."

Dottie nodded in agreement. There was nothing more to say. Words were meaningless when one is alone, deeply mired in one's thoughts, in the company of a friend.

"Well, better get going, it's Monday and you know what Monday night is," said Eugenia.

"More kids to watch and feed, just like the horses," said Dottie. She was referring to the weekly dinner that both women supplied on Monday evenings for Tom and Alex. "Can you imagine if Lorraine was still alive?" Dottie was referring to Tom's deceased wife and Alex's mother.

"You know rumor has it that she had Tom wrapped around her little finger. I didn't know her, but I heard she was something else."

"Hell, Lorraine had everybody wrapped around her little finger," retorted Eugenia. "When we were young, all she had to do was bat an eyelash and she'd get an A. Pissed me off. Tried it one day on the principal. Got detention." She scowled.

~

There was a loud roar outside and a large tractor loomed into view just outside the back door.

"Howard's here," said Dottie, referring to one of the local dairy farmers. "He's cleaning up my manure pile today. Taking it to put on his fields, I suppose."

Eugenia furrowed her brow and said, "Bull, he does. Takes it to ol' man Snyder for his asparagus beds. Gets paid handsomely for it too."

Dottie half smiled and said, "if he gets it out of here, I don't care what he does with it. He can grind it up and sell it for hamburger for all I care."

Eugenia laughed as booted feet stomped up the back steps.

"I'm heeeerrrrrrre," yelled a raspy, sing-song voice.

"Come in, Howard," said Dottie. "Want a sip of tea?"

"Don't touch the stuff," came the brusque retort. "But I'll take some of those there cookies," said Howard, stretching his neck and eyeing the plate on the table as he came through the screen door.

Howard stepped into the kitchen and said, "reminds me of my mom's kitchen, the smells and the wood stove." He was obviously in a reflective mood and Eugenia had never seen this side of him before.

"That is, when my father wasn't around," he continued. "Things changed when he was around. He could be a real son-of-a-bitch. He never smiled, don't know what she saw in him. To this day none of us kids can figure it out. Now with him retired and all, they're getting on better than when all of us kids were home. They're traveling too....beats me," he shrugged his shoulders. "I guess all of us kids just intimidated him. Well, I'll just grab a few cookies and off I go. Time's a wastin'."

Dottie handed him the plate and he extracted three of the cookies. He turned and walked out the door to his tractor.

"Nothing like the odor of barn," said Eugenia.

"You should smell me when I come in from the horses," said Dottie.

Eugenia smiled and nodded as she got up and walked out the door and across the yard to her house.

Chapter Twelve

It was a hotter than usual day in Mobile, Alabama. The air conditioning in the police building was working overtime, even though it was before noon.

"We're checking county records to see if our Mr. Sellers is still around these parts," said Nedo. "If he's our killer, how many more people has he done away with?"

Checking the national database was daunting for the assembled task force. Many questions were left unanswered. Garrett would be in his early fifties now. Was he a drifter or a family man? Where was he employed? All these questions but no answers and just a trail of bodies.

Back at the little house on the bayou, the stains on the little dress, the floor and bed covers was, indeed, blood. The two people found in the barrel in the barn were identified as Katherine Bell and Bradley Sellers. Although the body of Selma hadn't been found, four skeletal remains, all children, were discovered in total. All had been bludgeoned to death with a blunt object. Assorted animals, more cats than anything, were also found under the remains, which told the police and FBI that Garrett's killing spree started early and had accelerated from animals to people.

It didn't take too many more days to find exactly what they wanted to know about Garrett including pictures. But Garrett had an infinity for disappearing and not being found. His latest whereabouts was Arizona and so the task force headed there.

They landed in Phoenix the next day and headed for a single-story ranch house in a subdivision of a well-to-do neighborhood. The two men got out of the car and approached the house, looking in the windows and walking around it. A middle-aged woman approached them and asked them if they were interested in the house and that she would call the realtor if they wanted.

"No," they both said.

"Who owns it?" asked Nedo.

"The people that were here last just disappeared so it went into foreclosure. Got up in the middle of the night and they were gone. Nice couple. She had a small daughter." She hesitated. Nedo flashed his badge and she stared at it for a moment, not sure if she wanted to say anything more.

"Can you tell us anything about him?" said Dave.

"Well, creepy, real creepy. I mean she was genuine, a real peach. He was aloof and standoffish and there was just something about him, like meanness. Thought he knew it all," she said, hesitantly.

"Do you know where he worked?" asked Nedo.

"At home. He never went out. All his business was conducted on the internet. They had nice cars, the little girl went to a good school and all. Always dressed nicely." The woman looked thoughtful.

"Yes?" said Dave.

"Well, I just had a feeling like she, the wife I mean, was abused. He was quite verbal, ahh vocal. I heard him shouting at her occasionally. It wasn't pretty."

"Cops involved in anything here?" said Nedo.

"No, and I'm here all the time. My partner and I pretty much stay by ourselves," said the woman, her bleached blond hair bobbing in the sunlight as she emphasized every word she said. "We run a boutique downtown, but I'm the financial end of it and he's the people person."

"Is the broker local?" asked Dave.

"Yes, we both know her. Want me to call her?" she asked breathlessly.

"Yes," said Nedo. "I want to go inside."

It didn't take long before a large, light blue Cadillac parked in the driveway in back of Dave's rental car.

Dave was busy quietly walking around the grounds. He was looking, looking for anything that would tell him if one inch of soil was disturbed on any part of the ground. He was standing behind some shrubbery, near the pool in the backyard when a glint of something metal caught his eye. He walked over, bent down and picked up a small watch; a child's watch. It was relatively new and of good quality.

He shouted for Nedo and Nedo came running.

"You're like a friggin' bulldog," said Nedo. "That what we need to name you? Bulldog?"

Dave smiled and turned to the neighbor lady. "Any other children around, I mean before this family came?"

"No," she said. "House was built just before they bought it."

"Let's take a look inside then we'll see what's next," said Dave.

The realtor unlocked the door and they were assailed with the stale odor of *locked-up house*. But something else, and Dave couldn't put his head to it.

"Was the place cleaned before it was put up for sale?" he asked.

The realtor nodded.

"What about the possessions? Were there any left?"

"That would have been the bank's business. I do know they hired a local company to do any cleanup, but there wasn't much here when they got finished," the realtor told them.

"Who were they?" asked Nedo.

Nedo got the name and phone number and called the cleaning company.

"He'll be here in about ten minutes. Said he has something to tell us," said Nedo.

Both men looked at one another. This didn't look good.

A late model van pulled into the driveway ten minutes later. The van was dark green and the lettering "Benson's Cleaning and Trash Removal" was lettered in vivid pink along the side and back of the vehicle. A short middle-aged man jumped out and came up to Dave.

"Hi, I'm Les," he said "and I cleaned this here house out. What I wanted to tell you," he spoke in hurried, breathy, short sentences, "was that I cleaned up and then had to get a dumpster to haul out all the stuff. There was some fine things and I ended up taking some of them to a storage unit. There was jewelry too, but the bank said to dispose of it all. I mean, mighty fine things. They vacated in one hell of a hurry."

"We must have been on vacation when you came with the dumpster," the neighbor whined.

"Yeah," he drawled, "could have. Took me and my crew two days to finish the job."

"Notice anything funny," said Nedo, "like spills that were hurriedly cleaned up. Spots on the kitchen or bedroom floor?"

"Not really, although there was a mess on the bed in the master bedroom. The sheets were obviously washed and then they were just piled up on top of the bed, mattress covers and all. They smelled like laundry detergent, real clean, but they were really stained. I just chucked em' out."

Nedo and Dave looked at one another.

"Time to call the locals," said Nedo.

"Yeah. I want to see that spot in the garden; it's bothering me," said Dave, looking worried.

Turning to Les, Dave asked, "see any garden tools in the garage and I know this is a long-shot, but did any of them look used?"

"Funny you say that," said Les. "I found a shovel out by the pool, just laying there. Almost whomped me when I stepped on it wrong. Oh, there was a rake there too, leaning against the fence."

~

Several minutes later a squad car pulled up in the driveway and two local policemen got out.

"Hi," said Nedo shaking hands with them and making introductions all around. Dave got both officers up to speed and they too went through the house.

As Dave stepped onto the back patio of the house, he noticed something familiar. His stomach lurched and he gingerly picked up a rock from where it had been obviously thrown against the foundation of the house. The rock looked out of place from the other stones scattered around for landscape effect. It was darker in color, larger and rounded on one end. It measured about two inches deep and five inches across and probably weighed around one to two pounds. Nedo came out the door and stopped.

"Where in hell did you find that?" he asked.

"Right here," said Dave pointing to the side of the house.

"Bulldog at work again," muttered Nedo.

"I'd like a lab to take a look at this. His modus operandi is hitting people over the head with rocks," said Dave flippantly. He called for an evidence bag and handed it to one of the policemen.

"I'll get right on it," said the policeman. "Be right back."

The other officer stayed with them as they made their way over to a line of bushes separating the property.

"Hum," said the officer, a younger guy with blond hair and a crewcut, "I garden a lot and this soil has been worked more recently than the rest of the soil around this spot. Not much rain here so you can tell. Also, the topsoil is not on the top anymore, but buried."

Dave looked at him and said, "I noticed that too. Shall we?" he asked, nodding toward the ground.

"I'm game if you are," said the officer and they both got down on their hands and knees. Nedo handed them the shovel, but thought better of it for evidence's sake. Fingerprints?

The neighbor appeared with another shovel.

"I know where this came from," she said. "It's safe to use."

It was obvious that someone had recently worked the soil. Outside the hole, the soil was as hard as concrete but where it was recently dug, the going was a little better. They were down about three feet when the tip of the shovel hit something other than dirt. It was obviously a cloth or blanket of some sort. Pieces of ripped black trash bag came up from the hole with the tip of the shovel and with it a stench so overpowering that both Dave and the officer gagged.

"Call in, we're not going any further," said Dave. Nedo nodded.

The police chief, a lab van and several other squad cars parked in front of the house. A few local news vans were also part of the entourage. They were quickly relegated to the other side of the crime tape as soon as the officers were able to string it up.

The coroner was called in and a stretcher carrying the body of a small child, wrapped in a blanket was extracted from the hole.

"Question number one, where's the woman?" asked Nedo.

"I wish I had those sheets," said one of the lab techs. "We could match the blood samples with that of the girl and see if it's one and the same or two different people."

Dave nodded thoughtfully.

"That rock might give us some clues. And for what it's worth," said Dave thoughtfully, "maybe she went with him. She might have been docile and controllable enough, and she could have gone along with all this." But he was frowning. His face had a puzzled expression.

"Always makes you wonder doesn't it?" said another officer. "That little girl is probably about my daughter's age."

"I'll call in the dogs," said the chief.

Dave looked across the pool and saw what looked like a small utility shed. Obviously, it housed the pool motor, cleaning tools and chemicals. He gravitated toward it. Suddenly all was quiet. All eyes were on him as he jimmied the door open.

"I don't think you have to call the dogs," he said, closing the door on a large garbage bag tied with rope and bright blue para cord.

Over dinner with the police chief they compared notes and the transcripts and statements from the neighbor, the realtor and the cleaning crew.

"The thing is where is he headed to next?" mused the chief. "We have a good police sketch from the neighbor and tapes from the bank security cameras. That older sketch I'm sure is helping some so now we know what he looks like, but identity these days is easy to change. I'm checking into the foreclosure papers and the original mortgage applications and all that. Might get a clue there. As soon as I get the information, I'll get it to you."

"I still think we're missing something," said Dave. "Did you check out the identity of the woman?"

"Yes, she was a native of Shelby, Alabama," said the chief, a note of sadness in his voice.

"Oh!" said Dave, surprised. "That's about fourteen miles from Tomisina where he murdered his father, his father's girlfriend, a little girl and others. We think it's where his killing spree began."

The officer looked surprised.

"Could he be going after his childhood friends, enemies, anyone that pissed him off?" mused the chief.

"Our thoughts exactly," said Nedo.

"I need some time alone," Dave said quietly. "I'm going back to Alabama and I need to send for my son, Matt. I think he and I can come up with a profile of Garrett. He knew him probably better than I knew him. He and Matt were together for several years before Matt left his company."

"Ever have a real creepy feeling like the only one to make it out alive was Matt, and Garrett wants to finish the job on him?" remarked Nedo, thoughtfully.

"Thought about it," said Dave. "It does make sense that he could be a target, if he knew where he was."

Nedo was really quiet.

Differently Double

Chapter Thirteen

Gene felt calm, almost detached most of the time. He was content, read a lot, ran the antiques business for Mrs. Henshaw and fished some. Fishing afforded him an opportunity to meditate and now, here he was at the fishing hole near the falls in the back of the cemetery.

Two boys approached. He had seen them around. One was heavy and rather bookish looking and the other, who carried a fishing pole in one hand and a paper cup of worms in the other, was much smaller and darker than his partner.

"Hi," they both said in unison.

"We seed you around," said the smaller boy.

"Yeah, you're the guy who rides the bicycle," said the heavier boy, who Gene noticed held a book in his hand.

"Yeah, that's me," said Gene, laughing. "My name's Gene, what yours?"

"This here's Kenny and I'm Louis," said the smaller boy, extending his hand.

"Nice place to fish," Gene said. "Nice and quiet. My first time here. Is this your place? If so, I won't interfere."

"Naw," said Louis, "it's one of our favorite places besides the lake, but that's too far to walk today."

"I like the lake too," said Gene.

"We sneak in through the back way. We're not members of the Fish and Game Club," said Kenny.

"Well," said Gene, "you two can be my guests anytime you want. I'm a member and I'll put you on the list as my guests, that way you can go anytime you want and not be harassed. Heck, I'll even get you membership cards."

"Yeah!" said Louis. "That there Frank fellow, he checks you all out. Hollered at me once, so I ran."

"Frank's a good guy," said Gene, "I'll tell him you're both ok."

"Wow," said Kenny, "we really appreciate that."

"So, what brings ya here to this part of the world?" said Louis. "Heard you're from down south."

"Yes," said Gene. "I think I have relatives here somewhere and I'd like to find them." Their conversation about family brought him back to the one time he overheard his mom talking about her sister. His grandparents never mentioned her, but he knew someone was sending money from somewhere for his grandparents and mom to live on. With that one comment, the fact became cemented in his mind that he did indeed have an aunt. But where was she and was she still alive?

"Now that all of mine are gone, with the exception of a brother and maybe an aunt," said Gene reflectively.

"A brother?" said Louis. "I have plenty of them. That's why I'm here. To get away from them all."

"You're lucky," said Gene, "but I haven't seen my brother since I was very little and it was good riddance when he and my dad left. I was raised by my grandparents and my mother. My mom disappeared one evening. Never saw her again. And when my grandparents passed, I went into the Navy. I got out, I went for the oil rigs and made good money and here I am. That was years ago." He '' and said thoughtfully, "and I'm an identical twin."

Kenny was mesmerized by Gene and said, "ya know, twins, especially identical ones, can feel one another's emotions if they're in tune with one another. At least that's what this book I'm reading here says."

Gene was curious. "What's the book?" he casually asked.

"It's on the pseudosciences and metaphysics. Time travel, emotional fields, energy theorem, ley lines..." He stopped when he noticed Gene was openly staring at him in disbelief.

"That's my interest. Pseudoscience and all. When I was in the Navy I went to college for physics and math but got out sooner than I should have."

"Wow," said Kenny, "you'll have to talk to Steve, the anthropologist in town. He's into it big time and a member of the club."

"The club? You mean the local paranormal club!" shouted Gene, trying to suppress his emotions.

"Yes. Our best friend Lydia, it's her gran and her friend that runs it. Why don't you just go to a meeting. It's once a month, but it rotates around.

They never seem to meet in the same place month to month. They take turns going to different members' homes," said Kenny. "I'll ask Lydia tomorrow."

Gene nodded his head.

They fished until dusk and then walked quietly through the cemetery and down the road toward their homes.

Differently Double

Chapter Fourteen

His mood changes were a terrible thing to see and then there was the problem with this dark spirit, the one that was with him; attached to him. It made him do things he knew were wrong, but that division between right and wrong was blurred many years ago. He was afraid of this spirit and it was getting more and more demanding the older he got.

He had loved his own mother dearly, but all she did was dote on his father and twin brother. That fueled a rage inside of him that made his resentment of them boil until he had no control. When his mother and brother walked out on him, there was nothing left but the rage and hatred he needed to fuel himself. He tried to give love but found that he just couldn't give of himself. He knew he had to right the wrongs in his life. There were still people out there he had to punish and kill. People who had abandoned him and the dark spirit within was always there to remind him of that fact.

~

Gene's sleep was troubled that night. He woke up several times covered in sweat. The dreams, the feeling of eminent doom in the pit of his stomach happened every few weeks now. It eluded him for years, that restlessness of boyhood, but now it manifested as fear, hate and rage. What was this? It only happened at night, during sleep, but it left him feeling strange, almost trance-like the following day. The dreams were always the same, someone or something coming to get him and just as his eminent death was about to happen, he would wake in a cold sweat. He never saw the face of his assailant, but he knew, deep within his core, just who it was.

Differently Double

September

Chapter Fifteen

Labor Day was gone and with its passing came the first day of school. Yellow school buses were seen parked at the diner where drivers congregated after morning runs.

Lydia and Olivia usually met at the school steps at approximately seven-thirty in the morning. They came from opposite directions and most times Lydia would be walking with others from her side of the village. Olivia usually walked with her crowd from the trailer park and they picked up Alex along the way. They didn't take the school busses, as they all lived close to the school, making riding the bus unnecessary. As both groups approached the school, Mr. Cornelia's bus was unloading. Hulk, one of the basketball team members and a good friend of Josh's, was exiting the bus followed by his sister, Christine. There was a wheeze from closing doors and the bus alarm quieted as the bus started into gear and began its ride back to the bus garage at the side of the school.

"I know, it's my prerogative, but I don't want to have this become a giant kerfuffle," Christine said to a girl that was walking beside her. Christine glanced at the entourage that came from the direction of the trailer park and when she saw Alex, her face brightened. He sheepishly looked at her and then away, the smile never leaving his face.

Lydia and Olivia both looked at Christine's retreating back.

"Kerfuffle? Bull," said Olivia with distain. "That's my word. She stole it!"

Lydia rolled her eyes and shook her head.

"In a way she's a lot like me," said Hulk as he joined them on the sidewalk. "If she has something to put time and effort into she's great. She likes to have causes, ya know, like the environment...social justice. Just the opposite from my parents. They get into heavy fights a lot, and I think that's why my parents favor her over me. She'll tell 'em all off. I won't. She took up the cause for Alex and that really motorized her."

"Motorized?" said Olivia.

"Well, motivated, only I like to use motorized," said Hulk, sheepishly.

Lydia just burst out laughing. "Love it," she said, "just love it. Kerfuffle and now motorized. What's next?"

Olivia just looked at her with disdain.

At that moment, a blue minivan pulled up to the curb, a handicap placard swinging gently from the rear view mirror.

"Wonder who that is?" remarked Olivia.

Before either could react, two boys and a girl emerged from the van. Alex came and stood quietly by the girls, and Josh, Olivia's brother, and several of his friends joined them.

"Must be the new people in town," Josh remarked.

"Ahhh, more victims," remarked Hulk.

"Not anymore," said Josh, "not for me. From now on, no more bullying."

"What fun is that?" remarked a short, bucktoothed boy who was also a member of the basketball team. They called him Shorty.

"Because I don't like to be that way anymore," said Josh. "Besides we have to put on a good show for Alex here."

Both boys looked at Alex curiously.

"Besides, with Alex on our side, we're going to state sectionals this year."

"Bull," said Hulk.

"Dream on," said Shorty, sarcastically.

Alex just looked at the two boys with a semi-smile on his face.

"You a senior this year?" asked Hulk.

Alex shrugged his shoulders.

"Real world or college?" asked Shorty.

"I don't think BOCES has anything more to teach him and he wants to go into business with his father," said Josh.

"You don't mean Tom?" said Shorty.

"This the kid they all been talking about?" asked Hulk.

Alex, somewhat taken aback, looked from Josh to Shorty to Hulk and back.

"I think ol' Miss Goodwin put him in regular curriculum," commented Hulk.

The mom, the two boys and the little girl were approaching the small group. The woman held the hand of the girl who was obviously having a temper tantrum.

"Well," said Josh, "let's start a new leaf," as he approached the small group with Alex in tow.

"Anything we can do to help you?" Josh asked, his emphasis on the *we*.

The mom, looking quite harried, shook her head. "My two boys are in the seventh and eleventh grades and their sister wants to go with them and not to her own school."

Josh nodded as he noticed that the little girl obviously had Down syndrome.

"Is she enrolled at the Tow Path School?" asked Hulk, alluding to the State School and living facility for Down syndrome patients several miles away.

"Yes, and she doesn't go anywhere without the boys or me. This will be a first time," answered the mother.

Shorty said, "Wow, that's really tough. I can't imagine how she's feeling."

"Hey, my sister is just over there, she'll help out with the boys, I'm sure," said Josh.

"Appreciate it," said the mom.

Suddenly the little girl's hand reached out and grabbed Hulk's hand. Hulk look chagrined.

"Do you know anything about Down syndrome?" asked the mother.

"Very little," said Hulk. "I guess she knows I want to be a doctor," he said, quietly.

Alex just stared, intrigued. He had never seen anyone with this condition before.

"Yes, this is Doctor Hulk," said Shorty, with a snicker.

"Oh, come on, not out of the question," retorted Hulk, anger in his voice.

"Yup, you're just going to have to get over clumsy," said Josh.

"Yeah," said Hulk, resigned, "These are just not delicate operating tools yet," looking at his enormous hands.

They all laughed.

They found out that the little girl's name was Mandy and she was now openly staring at Alex and fidgeting with her foot. And unknown to them, a small crowd was gathering on the sidewalk. Josh spotted Olivia and shouted, "Hey sis, these boys are new. Wanna show em' around?"

Olivia, Lydia and Kenny came forward and introduced themselves.

"Hey twerp," said Hulk to Kenny.

"Alright," said Josh, "none of that. In fact, I'd be real nice to Kenny if you wanna pass advanced chemistry. He's smarter than ten of you."

Kenny's face turned red and he turned away and started walking toward the school.

"No shit," said Hulk. "Hey kid, wait up, I wanna talk to you. How good are you at chemistry?" is the last thing Josh heard.

~

Kenny stood across from Hulk, not far from the front entrance to the school.

"I don't like being called twerp" Kenny said, a note of brevity in his voice.

"Ok, old habits die hard," said Hulk, a look of resignation on his face.

"By the way," said Kenny, hesitantly, "what's your real name?"

"Promise not to tell anyone?" said Hulk.

He put his hand on Kenny's arm and squeezed.

Kenny looked straight at him and then down at his now aching arm.

Hulk removed his hand slowly, a look of resignation on his face.

"You, sir, have an issue with self-worth," said Kenny, getting braver by the moment.

"I didn't come here to get psychoanalyzed," said Hulk. "I get enough of that shit at home."

"Why," said Olivia from behind him. "Your mother and father hate you that much?"

Hulk sat heavily on the bottom step of the wide front entrance of the school. "Yeah, I'm the thorn in their side. I'm clumsy, stupid and worthless and I have empathy for people. Ok, sometimes I don't show it, but most of the time I really do feel compassion. My sister can do no wrong. They say I don't need an education if all I'm going to do is farm work or manual labor. They have my future all figured out, all I need to do is show up."

He continued, "I like people. I like helping them, but sometimes I take my problems out on others. Makes me feel good at the time and guilty afterwards. I love to talk with my gram, but now she's in a nursing home. My dad and mom never go to visit her. All they do is bitch and complain about how much money it costs to take care of her. They put her away and just forgot about her like a throw away package. I love my gram; she ran the farm before she got sick. Her and I were a team. I try to go see her once every few weeks, but I have to bum rides to get there, or walk."

He felt two hands on his shoulders and looked up to see Lydia standing over him. She sat down next to him and said, "I think you're a hero seeing your gram and all. It must be nice."

"Only time I get to have a decent conversation, where I can truly say what I want and be who I am," he said sadly.

"I'm lucky. I have a gram living here," said Lydia. "Although my dad and her don't see eye to eye occasionally. It's fun to be around them, just to see what one will say to the other. It's like a sparring match."

"Well, you asked me my name. Ok," sighed Hulk. "My name is Sylvester Henry Thornfield."

"Ouch, sounds like an English Lord," said Olivia who had been hanging onto the railing of the bottom step.

"What grade are you in?" asked Kenny.

"Eleventh," said Hulk. "They kept me back a year. I'm in the same grade as my sister, Christine." He said his sister's name as if spitting out the words. Olivia just rolled her eyes and let out a large sigh. Lydia glared at her.

"College is not out of the question," said Lydia thoughtfully.

"Ever hear of money," said Hulk.

"Ever hear of scholarships," sneered Olivia.

Chapter Sixteen

Police Chief Chris Edwards answered the phone at the Emeryville Station in upstate New York. A small town force of which Matt was one of the officers and an investigator.

"Matt's out on duty," said Chris when the secretary handed him the call.

"It's Dave," she said.

"Oh, our FBI man?"

The secretary nodded. She was older, more like the mother of the group and she loved her *boys* as she called them.

"Hey Dave, how's doings down in the sunny south?" asked Chris.

"More like how's the murders," said Dave. "We're uncovering some real bad ones and it's one man and this goes to family with one of your officers."

"How so?"

"Stepbrother of Matt," said Dave,

"Ahh shit. This affect you too, or am I wrong?"

"No, you're not wrong," said Dave, weariness in his voice.

"Listen, can you spare him for a week. I need his thoughts on this case and I have a very awful feeling this guy is coming after Matt and anyone else who would get in the way."

"Coming my way? Now wait a minute," said Chris.

"I'm afraid so, if my hunches are right."

"Ok, I'll get him on the next plane. Albany to Mobile, I think there's a direct flight."

"I'll make the arrangements," said Dave. "You want to break the news, or will I?"

"I'll go over now and you follow up."

"One other thing," said Dave, "this is not going to be a picnic for him. It'll bring back the murder of his sister and all the other shit from his early life. Won't be easy."

"Ok, I'm on my way," said Chris and hung up.

~

Olivia and Lydia rode their bikes to Miller's crossroads and back, over the bridge, past the cemetery and noticed someone walking on the side of the road.

"Hey," they said in unison, "Where ya going?"

"I was just fishin," said Louis. "Caught some bass, but I like going down by the falls in the back of the cemetery. Peaceful back there. Kenny likes to go with me and read; I likes to think and fish."

They walked back into town together.

"Well, see you tomorrow," said Lydia to her two friends.

Olivia went on with Louis, as Lydia walked her bike up her driveway. Lydia sauntered past the police car. Her father would be home now. As she parked her bike, she heard voices in the kitchen and one of them was not her father nor her mother. Her penchant for eavesdropping was monumental, so she quietly creeped up the back stairs to the open back door and stood there.

Chris was sitting opposite Karen and next to Matt.

"I have a request, well ahh, it's more like an order. The FBI needs a man and you're it," said Chris.

"What do you mean?" asked Matt, brusquely.

"You're being sent to help them on a very important case."

"What does it have to do with me? I mean, they have hundreds in their ranks," said Matt defensively.

Suddenly Matt stood up, "just where is it I'm going?" he asked. His piercing gaze never leaving Chris's face.

Matt's voice had raised a little and Karen stood also. Matt motioned for her to sit.

"It seems that your brother ah, Garrett," said Chris, quietly "is at it big time. So far, they have several murders pinned on him and he ends up eluding everyone. They need a fresh perspective. Your perspective."

Chris watched Matt. His face was like a mask. He was silent and Karen had never seen him like this.

"Ya know, my mother did me a big favor by kicking me out of the house at sixteen. I think she knew what would have happened if I stayed," said Matt.

"You mean you'd be another victim?" asked Chris.

Matt nodded.

"His killing spree started when I was twelve, if not before. My little sister. I always knew he did it, but not how to prove it?" said Matt.

"They may have the answers now, but Dave is afraid," said Chris.

"Afraid?" questioned Matt.

"He'll explain when you get there," sighed Chris.

Lydia was spellbound. She had had an aunt, a real aunt, but she was murdered. Wait til the gang hears this. She shifted her weight and banged against a broom sitting near the railing. The racket it made when it fell made everyone's head turn to see what it was. Lydia was humming to herself as she bent to pick it up.

"I'm home," she chirped.

Her father looked at Karen and they both were wondering the same thing; how long had she been standing there?

Just then the phone rang. It was Dave.

"Hi," he said, cautiously.

Matt didn't speak for a few seconds then tersely said, "when?" as he put the phone on speaker.

Ignoring the question, Dave said, "I'm sending some pictures to you. I want you to give them to Karen and let Lydia and her friends see the ones of him now. It's a composite with and without facial hair. I don't know how far this could go, but he's killing all across the south. What I saw today makes me want to retire real fast. This guy is insane and we have to stop him. You are the only living person that really knows him, his quirks, his idiosyncrasies. You are invaluable to this investigation," said Dave.

"You got the fax number?" Matt asked, tersely.

"Yeah, sending now," answered Dave.

Lydia sat down slowly on one of the kitchen chairs.

The phone rang in the small office Karen used, off the hallway to the living room.

"They're there now. The first one maybe you saw it at one time, maybe you didn't. The other ones are recent sketches."

"Has he gained any weight?" asked Matt.

"Not according to the neighbors at the scene today," said Dave.

"I don't want to know," Matt retorted putting his head in his hands

"No, you don't," said Dave quietly.

It was momentarily quiet in the small kitchen, the silence like a shroud over everyone sitting there.

"Alright," sighed Matt, "when?"

"Man's on the way now," said Dave.

"What?" they all said in unison.

"Yes, within the hour you'll be on the plane and headed toward Mobile."

"You owe me a year of raws for this. Dammit," Matt said.

Dave just laughed and hung up.

"What are raws Dad?" asked Lydia.

"Raw oysters sweetie," Matt answered.

"EEEEik," said Lydia, her mouth open in a sneer.

"I got a man patrolling here and I think that the gang should be alerted," said Chris.

Karen nodded and quietly said, "I'll take care of it."

"I figured you'd know who to see," said Chris.

"I'll see the school principal tomorrow too," said Karen.

"Good idea," said Matt quietly. "I better get packed. You guys stay here and talk. Look at the photos."

Karen went to the office and retrieved the photos.

"My, handsome young man that father of yours," she said as she handed the copy of the faded photo to Lydia.

"He was fat," said Lydia.

A man with a very narrow face and high cheekbones stared out of the next photos. One depicted Garrett with hair, another with a mustache and another with no facial hair at all.

Karen stared at them. "I'm getting vibes from these, vibes I just don't like," she said. "And, he looks very familiar, but how? I just don't know."

Matt, coming back into the kitchen glanced at the sketches and his stomach tightened, for there was the exact image of Bradley, his deceased mother's boyfriend staring back at him.

She quietly sat them down on the table and Lydia picked one up.

Matt came back into the kitchen.

With a resigned look on his face he said, "Study them and show them to all your friends. Anyone sees him, let the police know right away."

There was a beep of a horn outside and Matt let out a deep sigh and looked at his wife. He looked like he was going to cry.

"I'll be back in a few days," he said as he wrapped his arms around Karen, and then bent to give his daughter a kiss on the forehead.

Chris walked out with him.

"Take care of them," is all Matt said as he placed his small suitcase in the back seat of the car and hopped in front.

Differently Double

Chapter Seventeen

It was sunny and warm as Karen made her way down the sidewalk, past the school and onto Maiden Lane. Dottie and Eugenia were on Eugenia's porch having tea and scones. She walked up the sidewalk to the rear porch with a sheaf of papers in her hands. She sat down heavily on the worn metal porch furniture.

"You look like you're pissed or on a mission," commented Dottie.

"I have here a composite sketch. Several of them," said Karen, breathlessly.

"A what?" said Eugenia.

"A picture done by a police artist showing a man that all police units in the US are looking for. He's dangerous and a killer. Please show these to as many people as you can. I understand he is headed this way."

She showed the pictures to both women.

Eugenia looked at the pictures and passed them to Dottie, who just stared. Dottie's brow was wrinkled and she said, almost to herself, "Looks like someone I went to school with."

"Now Dot," said Eugenia, turning to face her.

"No, seriously, he's a dead ringer for a boy I used to know in school. A real wiseass. I remember his daddy, a real nice man, had a catfish business on the bayou."

"Remember his name?" Karen asked.

"No," said Dottie, abruptly.

Karen, taken aback by her quick answer and the feeling she got that Dottie wasn't exactly telling the truth said, "I think you should talk to Matt about this."

"Yeah, but maybe it's a relative," said Dottie, obviously not wanting to talk anymore. Her face was scarlet red and Eugenia never saw her this flustered before.

As Karen left, Eugenia looked inquiringly at her friend.

Sighing heavily Dottie said, "I think I just saw Banquo's ghost."

Differently Double

Chapter Eighteen

The entire basketball team sat on the lower section of the bleachers.

"Ok," yelled Coach. "Some new players and we'll have tryouts, so let's play a little basketball and see how we do. I don't want any bitching about where and how I assign you. Some of you need to be reassigned."

Josh, team captain, stood up and introduced the two new boys.

"This here's Alex, he's a senior...I think." This comment elicited laughter from the group and an eye roll and head shake from Alex. "This guy is a shooter, a long distance shooter," Josh continued. "He can put it in at long distances." This elicited several snickers from the group of boys.

"Ok," said coach, "get your minds out of the gutter."

"And this little guy is Charlie; we just call him Junior or JR and he is fast, real fast, and he gets around the court like a dynamo. I'm hoping that this year is our year. We haven't made a county, let alone a state tournament in decades."

"Hope springs eternal," muttered coach. "Let's play some ball."

Differently Double

Chapter Nineteen

Dave parted the curtain and looked out on the shimmering heat erupting from the pavement. He looked at the Gulf of Mexico in the distance and the pelicans that glided toward pilings that afforded them safe havens in the bay. Gulls swooped in the air overhead, chatting noisily. Matt came and stood with him. The officer from Emeryville, NY and the FBI profiler, father and son, both giving themselves a reprieve with the view.

Leonard DeVille entered the room. Sargent DeVille was of slight build but unnaturally tall with long, steel grey hair, worn in a ponytail. His face was narrow and his vivid blue eyes were so intense that some had to look away from his stare. He sported no facial hair. His was a kindly face that belied his thirty-plus years on the force.

"The two people in the barrels are safely in the morgue. They've been in their tombs a long time. But I still need to interview you, Matt," DeVille said.

Matt shook his head and smiled sadly. "Yeah, no problem."

"Looks like we have a serial killer and I say this carefully. There are lots of unsolves here, but I can't pin them all on him, if we can pin any at the current time," said DeVille.

"If it's him," said Matt, "no one's safe, especially the ones involved with him. Tracking him will be difficult. I mean, he's a drifter. He's smart enough to be under the radar all these years, but who else has he killed?"

Dave said, "we can start with court records. Especially the ones from the inquest when Sadie went missing. Then check into my child support and alimony payments to see where the checks were cashed. I stopped my payments for child support when Matt turned sixteen and left the house. I just want to kill that bastard lawyer that I'd hired at the time. But, he's dead. He really screwed me out of my family."

"Ok, that's a start. I know you have the national database on the case and fingerprints, see what we can come up with," said DeVille. "And yes, put it on the television, that most wanted show, plus *Facebook* and *Twitter*. We have a tip line and the calls are coming in. There's lots of leads, maybe one will pay off."

Dave nodded.

"Did he ever physically see you, I mean Garrett?" asked DeVille, turning to Dave.

"He saw me at the inquest when Selma, my daughter, went missing. He and Matt were both there. It's all starting to come back now. Garrett had this shit-eating grin on his face and I remember all I wanted to do is crawl over those seats and wipe it off his damned face."

"Remember anything else?"

"Not now, but remember, he's a real manipulator. A real bullshitter. He can weasel his way in anywhere. That's one thing we have against us, his ability to fit in."

"And," said Matt, "he's a very angry person. Very volatile."

"He ever try to harm you, Matt?" DeVille asked.

Matt shook his head no. "I was scared of him, never turned my back on him. He was older and he was diabolical. But, why wait this long to find me? It's been years."

"Honing his skills," Dave said quietly, closing the slats of the blind he was looking out of.

"There's something more, I can just feel it," Matt answered.

"Well, we got fingerprints from the barrel. He's careful on everything else. Started the nationwide database. We're matching them to the girl's body and the prints inside the pool shack, and that rock by the back door. Oh, there was one spot of blood on that rock. Matches the little girl's," said DeVille.

"The neighbor is at the precinct in Arizona now giving a detailed description to the police forensic artist on what he looks like. Should have a proof soon. He really doesn't look too much different than the other composites," he said.

Matt smiled sadly. "What makes a kid, a man do things like that? What could possibly have gone wrong in his life to make him that way, or was he born that way? I know his life wasn't easy, the beatings and all. And let's face it, my mother was no picnic to live with either."

Chapter Twenty

He investigated other Matt Bells in the areas he lived in, but all dead ends. Something was nagging at him, something his father's girlfriend said; the name of Matt's father.

What did he do...policeman...naw. Maybe? No, FBI; that's it FBI. He smiled quietly to himself.

That last Matt Bell was a favorite, a pre-teen. He would wait, for waiting was half of the game and then the attack. Ahhhh that careful, choreographed element of surprise.

~

"I have a gut feeling he's after you and me and our families. Just a gut feeling," said Dave quietly. "So, from Arizona to where now? I have a strange feeling he's hunting all the Matt Bells he can find, and anyone else who gets in his way."

"Yeah," groaned DeVille.

"Get into that database and find out all the Matt Bells who have been assaulted, murdered, kidnapped or gone missing in the last say... ten years. Maybe that will be a clue as to where he's been. Any unsolves, any age, all Matt Bells," said Dave.

"Our town of Emeryville has been in the news lately, so it won't be hard to find me or Dave," said Matt, sullenly. "We were interviewed enough and all over the news and even in the New York Times."

Nedo, Dave, Matt and several other officers including DeVille were all sitting around the chief's desk.

"So, you think his killing spree started early," mused DeVille.

"I know he used to kill birds and then small animals and he would pick on and punch little kids. He was a bully, but sometimes he would just sit quietly, like he was waiting, contemplating. It was like a light switch would turn off or on. Maybe it was bipolar or schizophrenia or whatever. His eyes were another thing. I could always tell when he was *going off*, as I used to call it. His eyes would go from a hazel green to almost black," said Matt reflectively.

Nedo produced a piece of folded paper and opened it to reveal a photograph and held it close to his body, face inward.

"I also found this in another drawer, out at the crime scene. I didn't want to show it to you until the right time." He slid it across the desk where it stopped in front of Matt. It was the photo of him and Sadie. Scrawled across the margin of the photo in blocky printing, a little faded but still legible, was the inscription *i got her – now I git you.*

Fingers of fear tickled Matt's neck and knotted his stomach. He handed the photo to Dave who nodded. Dave put a hand on Matt's shoulder and in a sullen voice said, "your mother did you a big favor; she booted you out. I think deep down, she knew what was coming. Have to give her credit for that."

Matt nodded silently, still reeling from the photograph and the cryptic message it held.

"My family's in danger, aren't they?" Matt asked quietly.

Dave nodded. "We'll be returning real soon," he said.

"Yes," said Nedo, "and I guess I'll be coming along. Again."

Dave, Nedo and Matt stepped out into the balmy afternoon.

"I need something to eat," said Matt.

"Me too," said Dave. "How about it, Brian?"

They all agreed.

"Let's go to Felix's down on the bay," said Matt.

It was late afternoon when they arrived at the fish camp. Climbing the long stairs to the first floor, (the building was built on twenty foot pilings), they entered the restaurant and were seated at a table overlooking the bay.

Matt ordered white fish, raws and seafood chowder plus sweet tea. Dave had the blackened tuna, fried okra, crab cakes plus a beer and Nedo had the same.

Dave looked at his son. "You ok?"

"Good as I can be. I'm letting go. Let go let God as the girls tell me. I imagine things are tense at home right about now. The pictures have been circulated. They all know."

"Yeah," said Nedo with resignation in his voice. "And I can imagine all the spells and incantations being cast as we speak." He shook his head slowly from side to side and smiled a slight smile. "Back into the never-never world we go," he said lightly.

Matt smiled at him and then burst out laughing.

Dave nodded and smiled. "Might do some good, you never know, Brian."

"You still have to tell me about my grandmother the witch," laughed Matt as he glanced sideways at Nedo.

Nedo just stared at him.

Dave smiled, nodded and said, "that's for another time, but I'm sure Lydia and Eugenia would like to hear about her too. You said you have one more place to go?"

"Yes," said Matt, "back to the scene of the crime; the house. Something's pulling me."

"Funny you should say that, I feel the same way," said Dave, his brow furrowed.

"Early tomorrow morning and then we'll be on the two pm plane back home," said Matt.

"I have paperwork to finish and the team to gather. We'll all meet in Emeryville day after tomorrow," said Nedo.

They finished their meal, ordered coffee and sat staring at the sunset over Mobile Bay. The sky was semi overcast, but the multitude of pinks and blues made a palette to delight any discerning eye. Gulls swooped and soared on the eddying currents of air as the unceasing waves washed onto the shore.

Differently Double

Chapter Twenty-One

Matt drove the rental car to the old house. Crime scene tape still fluttered in the slight breeze coming off the bay. They headed up the weedy driveway.

Dave, deep in his thoughts, contemplated about the last time he saw his daughter. It was not a nice time. Sadie had seen him and came running down the driveway into his arms. That was the last time he saw her alive.

He remembered the deep and raspy voice that came from the vicinity of the top step of the front porch. "What in hell do ya want?"

"See my daughter is all," he had said. "After all I have a right too."

"Well, no more if I kin' help it," said Katherine, his ex-wife.

"Tis quite a place," he said, conversationally.

"It's my man's place. His sister's. But it's ours now. None of your business...it is....we just moved in. But none of your son-a-bitchin' business."

Dave turned to go and overheard a voice behind him, a deep guttural voice full of menace and hatred. He turned to see a man, tall and very thin with brown hair streaked with grey.

Dave nodded, "just here to see my kids."

"You don't see anybody ya hear," said the man and Dave looked into eyes so full of hatred and coldness he shivered.

Shot back into the present, he thought "Why, oh why didn't I get those kids of mine out of there? Why?"

When he confronted David Bowmaker, Esquire, his lawyer at the time, he was told that he was working on it. Three weeks later his daughter is missing and assumed dead and several years later Bowmaker is dead and a nationwide manhunt is out for the man's wife. But her trail grew cold and still remains, to this day, a cold case in Alabama State Police files. I bet he would have sold his mother for his gain. Yes, always looking over his shoulder that guy. Even when he saw him in court the rumor was how many judges could good ol' David buy off today? "Someday," he mused, "someday I will pursue this case a little more."

Matt sat on a small pile of rocks in front of the house. A rusty flagpole stood at the center of the pile which at one time had obviously been a rock garden. For an instant Matt saw an elderly lady, slight of build and stooped, tending her flower garden in an old floral print dress. "How often do you come here?" he muttered, "or haven't you left yet?"

Matt looked up to see his father making his way toward the small garage, next to the house. Deep early morning shadows crossed the old driveway, now choked with weeds. He looked back and memory upon memory of an earlier life flooded over him. Then it started, a motion picture that you have to watch...must watch. He couldn't turn away. He saw the raging fight between the man and the woman. There in the shadows was a tall, lean boy, the boy Garrett. Rage was everywhere, it assailed him in waves, he shivered but he watched, he couldn't turn away. Slowly the boy raised his arm and slammed the rock he was holding into the side of the man's head. The man crumpled onto the floor; the woman screamed and ran out the back door, fear giving wings to her feet. She headed for the dock at the rear of the property, but Garrett didn't follow, not just yet.

With trembling fingers, the woman started to untie the knot that held the boat fast to the dock. This just might be her freedom. She felt him first, that evil that permeated him. She didn't turn to face him; she clawed furiously at the knot in the rope and then she heard a hollow ringing sound at the back of her head, and she fell into darkness.

Matt wasn't shaken by the vision, just saddened. He was relieved that his mom wanted to share her story with him.

He felt a hand on his knee and there was his mother sitting on the grass beside him. She didn't look at him, she just stared at the ground. "Thanks for showing me that, Mom," whispered Matt, tears coming to his eyes.

She looked up at him now, a small, sad smile on her face.

"I love you. I know Dad understands and now, as my mother-in-law would say, it's time to take the hand of the angel and go. There are lots of people waiting for you. It's a lot better life over there than it was here. There's nothing more here. You've found me and I understand."

A ray of sunlight fell on the place where they were sitting and with it a blinding flash of light lit up the small area. Matt was filled with an understanding, the depth he never felt before.

"I guess I'm gonna have to hang around the gang a little more," he muttered, meaning his wife's and Eugenia's paranormal group.

~

Dave stood in the small, overgrown driveway about twenty feet from the small garage. The garage sat empty, the doors gone, it's maw open like a cavern ready to swallow all who dared enter. He looked at the overturned barrels, all empty and thrown on their sides, scattered in the police quest for more bodies and evidence.

Approaching the garage, he stood there looking in and then he noticed in one corner of the dark interior a small pink, straw hat. A child's hat. He smiled and started to enter the garage when he saw movement in the back yard. He walked toward it and into a weedy area. He could see an old dock in the distance but because of Hurricane Katrina, no more water flowed there. The downed trees and brush made a barrier in this area. An old boat was tied to the dock and he headed for it. The ground was muddy, but there were still vestiges of a path.

Then he noticed the small form just ahead of him. She was skipping along the path, chasing butterflies and laughing to herself. The sunlight momentarily shone on the small form in the little sundress and she turned to face him, a curious look on her face. Fifty feet separated them and his heart was filled with such longing he thought he would crumple to the ground. A tiny voice said "I'm here to help. Mama's gone, but I'll help."

He now understood Matt's pull to this place. He knew that his dead wife had come to Matt for he now felt her presence also. Dave approached the dock and there it was, like an egg in a nest of weeds; a rock. An oval rock. Out of place, yes, but there it was.

"This is where she met her end," said Matt in a quiet voice from behind him.

Dave nodded and pointed toward the rock on the ground.

"Yes, that's how she died," said Matt." That's what she wanted to show us."

Tears coursed down Dave's face as Matt put his arm around his shoulder.

"It's time," Matt said quietly.

They turned and made their way to the car in the brightening light of the noonday sun.

Chapter Twenty-Two

"He's coming," said Mandy.

"Who's coming sweetie?" asked her father.

"He's coming. Must be ready," she repeated.

She was picking up stones that neatly fit into her hand and was carefully placing them on piles next to the driveway.

"Who Mandy?" his voice quietly probing.

"The Dark Man," she said in a hushed, frantic whisper. "He's coming."

Differently Double

Chapter Twenty-Three

The crowd was assembling for the first game of the season. The gymnasium at Emeryville Central School was packed tonight. Most people in town felt sorry for the basketball team and always showed up to support its flailing attempts at winning a game.

It didn't matter that Emeryville was playing their most competent rival, the multi-titled Masonville High. Masonville was a large school eleven miles north and light years ahead in league championships and titles, making it into the finals every year. Little Emeryville didn't have a chance. Well maybe...slightly...with a lot of prayers...!

"Well, lookey who's here? Surprise, surprise! My mom and my dad," groaned Hulk.

Josh came up to him.

"Listen," he said, "you are a genius on the court so let's all get with it. We're going to win tonight."

"If we don't," mumbled Hulk, "I'll hear about it all this week, next week and beyond. Into eternity for sure. Like all the other times."

Coach had carefully schooled every member of the team over the past weeks to work as a unit. During practice, coach had shut out all onlookers so he could school the boys individually on strengths and weaknesses. This was a new team with a new attitude and a new direction. No more individual shooters that had dominated the team's offense and defense before, but a schooled unit, one where every team player knew what the other would and could do. Instead of taking an antacid after each and every practice and game, Coach now shared a renewed enthusiasm and it showed in every boy on the team. Spirits were high.

Alex and Hulk, as well as Josh, turned out to be great team players. Snoopy and Gaggle, along with Tiny, Shorty and JR, were fast learning the new game plan and welcomed the renewed effort and spirit. JR, being one of the new kids, was more like the team mascot. But when allowed to play, he was faster than lightning down the court and could dribble the ball with the best of them.

The small gymnasium was now filled to capacity. At the start of the game Emeryville kept pace with Masonville so by the third quarter

Masonville had forged ahead by just ten points.

Masonville figured they would be the *Dragon Slayers* again this year and that Emeryville, a bunch of Guinevere's, would fall to the wayside just like every other year. But Masonville was noticing that something was different this year. They just couldn't figure it out. Attitude, cooperation and the fact that there were several players that were still sitting on the bench for the entire three quarters of the game. This was something that never happened with Emeryville.

Coach signaled to Josh who would now sit out the last quarter. Josh was learning, as was all his team members, that what mattered most was team effort not individualism.

Alex noticed that his father was sitting next to Hulk's parents who were guffawing and cat calling about letting Hulk play more. They had something to say about everyone's playing. Alex noticed by the look on his father's face that he was doing a *slow burn*.

Hulk looked at coach, embarrassed and said sadly, "my ol' man is here tonight and you can hear 'em from here. How embarrassing is that? Even my sister doesn't want to sit near 'em."

"I'll throw them out," said Coach, "if they become ornery. Just like I did the last time."

"No need to worry," said Josh, nonchalantly. "Look who they're sitting next to."

Coach looked and let out a laugh.

"Don't cross my ol' man," laughed Alex with a smirk on his face.

Fourth quarter and Masonville was ahead with a score of twenty to ten. Now the game was taking on new energy. Masonville's finest were out to annihilate Emeryville one last time and the first game of the season to boot. This game was just practice to them, or so they thought. Alex and JR were now in the game. Hulk had been sitting out the second and third quarters and now he was ready to go in again also. Alex and Hulk high-fived one another and headed for the court and their positions.

Hulk was relentless and so were his other team members. They managed to stop Masonville from getting any more points as they gained another four points on them. There was tension in the air as one after another of the opposing players were blocked by Hulk and his teammates. Then things started to happen. With half the fourth quarter now gone and the score twenty to fourteen, JR, lightning fast dribbled the ball to Hulk who passed it to Alex at half court. No one was paying attention to the tall, gangly boy with the unkempt hair. Alex was waiting, patiently and at half court the boy and the ball rose into the air as one. With great precision the ball continued its airborne journey toward the hoop. Swish, it was in and it took the crowd seconds before they realized just what had happened. There was a momentary stunned silence and then the eruption that took place in that auditorium was like that of a bomb going off at close range. Coach had trouble suppressing a smirk as he looked at the opposing team's coach who stood there with his mouth open, just gaping at Alex and then at JR and back to Alex.

~

Tom sat next to Hulk's parents and he endured the play by play and the cat calling until he had had enough. The last straw came when Bill, Hulk's father, stood up and screamed at the coach, demanding that Hulk take Alex's place and Josh come back into the game.

Tom stood up to his full height, turned and faced him. With a steady gaze he sneered, "leave 'em alone. You were the worst player on the team when we were growin' up. Leave 'em alone. That's my son play'n' and he stays play'n."

Tom turned and sat back down as Bill, Hulk's father, sat down with a thud. Before turning his head back to the game Tom glared at Bill's wife, who shrunk from his gaze.

Alex managed three more half-court shots into the hoop and several from the sidelines. The defense managed to take a good deal of pressure off Alex and offense did their job superbly by being able to fake shots and passing the ball here and there on the court with smug abandon. They managed to fool the other team enough so that in the end Emeryville won the game thirty-six to twenty.

When word got out the next day about Masonville's slaughter, all the local newspapers were aghast. The weekly paper in Emeryville was the only one who covered the whole game, along with pictures and interviews of the entire team. Richard Perry, the owner and editor of the local paper, was finally able to elicit envy from the other area newspapers with his play-by-play reporting of the game.

~

Alex was asked how he kept his cool on the court. He just shrugged and said, "I have lots of friends who meditate and I practice each day. I have learned to quiet my mind, so instead of running around the court on adrenaline and screwing up most of my shots, I relax and calm myself. I get there just as fast, but I'm not all hot and bothered."

Hulk, overhearing the conversation, agreed. He confided in Josh that he also used meditation to get away, in his mind from the *good ol' home front* with all the screaming and yelling. "I just shut the ol' man out," he stated.

Alex looked at his friend and teammate and said, "that's not meditating, that's being smart."

Chapter Twenty-Four

Nedo and his team, plus Dave and Matt, were back in Emeryville and working late. They were investigating photos of murder scenes. One woman was found in a crevice in a cliff in Tennessee and three more, a mom, a daughter and grandmother were found bludgeoned to death in a state park in Pennsylvania. No murder weapon but all blunt force trauma and they were now waiting for the official coroner's reports.

"We have pics at the scene in Pennsylvania. Apparently one of the vics had her cell phone operating," said one officer. "Take a look here."

Nedo looked at them and his stomach fell. "I need a drink," he said sarcastically.

One of his men, a man known as Norton, just looked at his boss and smiled a knowing smile. He was here the last time they visited Emeryville, not too long ago.

These were pictures of a campsite, a little blurry but still discernible. In one of them was the figure of a shadowy, tall man and just behind and to the left of him was another figure, the figure of a small girl in a summer dress. The problem with the small girl was that you could see right through her into the darkened forest beyond with its play of light and dark on the trees. The girl looked like a double exposure. The figure of the little girl showed up in all of the pictures but two. One picture showed a young teenage girl and there was the little girl, partially visible on the left side of the photo and again you could see partially through her.

"Here we go again," sighed Nedo to no one in particular.

The following day, Matt was busy doing paperwork at his desk and Lydia had decided to visit him at the station after school.

"What's this?" she asked.

"Pics of a murder scene and you don't need to see them," said her father, sternly.

"Are they gruesome?" said Lydia, a note of anticipation in her voice. Her eyes were bright.

"No, just crime scenes. Well, rather people at the crime scene before they were killed," remarked Matt, absently.

Lydia glanced at the first picture.

"Wow," she said, "that looks like the girl I see lately."

Her father glanced sideways at her.

"What do you mean?" he asked sternly.

"Well, the girl in the little summer dress. I see her every once in a while, now. Like she's around to protect me."

Matt's stomach grew queasy.

"Have you told this to anyone else?" he asked in a resigned voice, his face now resting in his hands as he looked squarely at his daughter.

"Just O," Lydia said flippantly, referring to Olivia.

Dave came up behind them. He took the picture from Lydia's hand and looked at it.

He smiled sadly and remarked, "well, as your mom says, help is always available from the other side if we ask for it."

Matt heaved himself from his chair, grabbed the photo and headed out the door.

~

"Ok, ok, you say your daughter sees this girl?" said Nedo, speaking with Matt in the station conference room.

"Yes, she told me she has seen the girl."

"When?"

"She really wouldn't open up to me. She just said, she has frequently seen her within the last few weeks."

Nedo sighed and looked at Chris. "Another ghost tale," he said sarcastically.

Chris nodded and said, "stranger things have happened, Brian. You know yourself with the last incident here."

Dave came through the door. Overhearing some of the conversation he said, "maybe I can give you some explanation on this. When Matt and I were down in Alabama, we took one last trip to the house. The crime scene. It was the morning of our flight out. My daughter Sadie, the one murdered by Garrett, at least we think it was probably his first human victim, she was there. A lot was revealed to both of us that day and Sadie did say she would be here to help, or words to that effect."

Nedo started to speak, but Dave held up his finger and continued.

"Whatever it is you believe, I don't care. But I do know what I heard and what I saw. Now gentlemen, we have a killer headed this way so let's go catch 'em."

Dave turned and walked out of the room.

Differently Double

Chapter Twenty-Five

He remembered the afternoon when he killed his father and his father's girlfriend. The sound of rock hitting bone. There was a terrible tremor within him the moment his father slipped to the floor, blood gushing from the wound at the side of his head. At that moment he heard a voice, a sneering voice whisper "atta boy, you're mine now."

He spun around and saw nothing; nothing but the retreating figure of his father's girlfriend. He named her the "cursing bitch." Coarse, boastful and mean, that was the woman who was Matt's mother.

Matt's life was no picnic either, "but we were so different," he mused. Why? She treated Matt like shit and where his own father was concerned, he all but ignored Matt, almost as if he was "off limits." His father took out everything on him, Garrett. "I'll make you a man yet," he would yell to the crushed and broken shell of a boy who cowered in the corner after an exceptionally brutal beating.

~

It was lunch break and several of the children were outside near the ball field sitting on the lawn. They were enjoying the sunshine before afternoon classes began.

Kenny laid on his back and with a deep sigh said, "ever look at clouds?"

Hulk, who was sitting near him looked up and grimaced. Kenny was tutoring him in physics.

"Lots of cloud movement," said Kenny. "Look, I see a sheep."

"Sheep my ass," said Hulk, glancing up from his textbook.

Alex, Josh, Olivia, Lydia and some of their classmates joined them.

They all sat down and then began to lie down on their backs, gazing up at the clouds. The air was pleasant now, but they all knew that soon they would all be bundled in heavy wool and fleece jackets and hats and gloves. Several of the kids played with their *iPads* and others were on their phones, while some just wanted the peace and quiet without all the gadgets.

"Ever look at clouds?" repeated Kenny.

"Look, there's a duck," exclaimed Olivia.

"Duck my ass," grumbled Hulk, now closing his textbook and looking skyward.

"Well, what do you think it is?" said Olivia tersely.

Moments later more kids showed up and in a short time they were all lying on their backs, looking at the clouds.

"Imagine my father asking me what I-I d-d did at school today," said Alex. "And I told him I was lying on the gr- gr- grass looking at clouds."

Josh burst out laughing. "Holy crap, I wanna be there when that happens," he said.

This elicited chuckles from most of the group which was growing in size by the minute.

~

Seth, one of the teachers at the school, came hurriedly into Principal Amy Goodwin's office. He rushed past the receptionist and stood at Amy's large, wooden desk.

She looked up at him as he said, "I really think you should see something from the vantage point of the second floor window and see it now. It will be worth your time, I swear."

Amy rose and followed him, her red high heels clicking on the over-polished floor of the hallway.

Seth entered his classroom and went straight to the window, which was open to the early fall afternoon. Amy sidled up beside him and looked down.

She looked at the scene below and then looked at Seth. She smiled, turned and walked out of the classroom.

A few minutes later Amy stood at the periphery of the circle of reclining students. She was mesmerized with the banter between students of all ages, lying in the grass looking at, of all things, clouds.

"Hey, I'm going to text this pic to my friends. They won't believe it. It looks like my dog," said one student.

"Yeah, great idea," said another.

"Wow what a pic," said another.

"We could form a cloud club," interjected a tenth grade student. "Then maybe I could get a passing grade in science."

Lydia was following one particular, sinister looking cloud when she just happened to glance at her neighbor. All she saw was a pair of high-heeled red shoes and she let out an audible gasp.

Bodies rolled and scrambled to upright themselves as they all stood to look at Miss Goodwin who now stood several bodies into the circle.

"I do agree about the duck," she said quietly. "I would like to recommend this to the entire school at least once a week. Lunch recess, gardening, meditation, cloud watching, relaxing. Stress is so overrated."

The kids started to clap and high five one another as a broad smile moved across Amy's face.

"How about making a nature trail," shouted one of the sixth graders.

"All of you could go in front of the school board and propose it. Good practice and it will help you upperclassmen with the governance class," said Amy. "You can all get the ball rolling."

"Can we make a boardwalk in the swamp?" asked a little girl.

"Maybe," said Amy, "but let's start small. We can always add on later."

Differently Double

Chapter Twenty-Six

Father Munro, the local Catholic priest, was busy rearranging all the furniture in the rectory. The monthly paranormal group, of which he was an honorary member, would meet at the rectory tonight and he had to have enough seating for fifteen to twenty people. Members rotated venues and he was the venue for this evening's meeting. Everyone brought something to nibble on and he looked forward to the *picnic*, as he called it.

Father kept himself busy with all the Church matters required of him, including saying Mass on Saturday evening and Sunday morning and on all holy days. He also kept a regular schedule of hospital visits. Several days a week he went to the café for lunch where he met his good friend Rev. John from the Episcopal Church. One day a week found him visiting the barber shop for the coffee club where he had his own mug with his name on it. At the barber shop one had the distinct privilege of keeping up with events going on in the community. The remainder of his week was spent with various parishioners and friends, hearing confessions and counseling. Jim and Gloria for Friday evening and a good game of dominos or *Monopoly* after. Every third Thursday for dominos with some of the seniors at the meal site and Sunday afternoon, after Mass, always with the McCarthy's for a fabulous home-cooked meal unless there was an emergency.

Father insisted he clean the rectory himself while Ellen, a local parishioner, cleaned the church. She was always there picking up the altar linens for washing, watering the vast array of plants, which he insisted on having in the church, and helping with the daily routines. He also had a part-time secretary, Cathy, who kept him on track with appointments, schedules and assisting with the printing of the Sunday bulletin. He loved these people and this area of New York. It was varied and interesting for not only was he a priest, he was also a demonologist.

~

Gene, hat in hand, stood on the porch of the rectory and rang the bell. Father Munro came to the door and Gene introduced himself and asked if the meeting was being held and if he was at the correct house. Father nodded and held open the door, but before Gene could walk in the door, Eugenia came up behind him from the sidewalk.

"Well hello," she said, a note of surprise in her voice. "I didn't take you to be interested in our group."

"I am," said Gene. "I'm looking for someone or something. My interest is in the metaphysical, so here I am, if you would accept me as a member."

"Well," boomed Father, "come on in und meet the gang. Most of them are here, und I'm sure, that before the night is over, others will be staggering in und staggering out."

Gene entered the large living room area of the rectory.

There was a table pushed against one wall and the large living room was crowded. Several people were sitting on a huge couch and the rest sat in various seats scattered throughout the room.

Some people he remembered, like the tall, good-looking man they all called Steve. He had come to the shop one day looking for pink flamingos for the lawn.

"You can't get them at the hardware store anymore. I don't go to malls and there's none in the city either, so I figured I'd try you out. Guess I'd call them antiques," he had told him.

Eugenia hustled Gene into the entryway between the kitchen and the living room. Dottie met them and Eugenia introduced Gene to her.

"Yes, I think we've met," said Dottie cautiously, "but what's your last name?"

"Riley," he said, "Eugene Riley, but everyone calls me Gene."

No one but Eugenia saw the look of horror that crossed Dottie's face as she spun around and exited toward the kitchen to get tea from the stove.

Dottie was leaning against the stove when Eugenia entered. Dottie looked shell shocked. Eugenia took the kettle from Dottie's hand and sat it gently down on the burner.

Dottie spun around to meet Eugenia's gaze.

"That guy is my nephew," is all she said, in a hoarse voice. "My sister married a real asshole. Abusive and real mean. A nasty man. She divorced him. They had two identical twin boys; one went with her and the other went with the father. As far as I know, neither boy has seen the other since. I know my pa would have killed his father if he showed up anywhere near us. My ma and pa were poor dirt farmers. Pecans, sweets, some tobacco, corn, beans, peanuts and some fruits. I got tired of it and left. Hell, I was the wild one. I wanted more and I got it, I guess. Yes, life happens and the rest is history, so they say."

Eugenia hugged her friend. "You don't have to say anything," she said.

Dottie nodded and said, "let's see how this plays out. The picture that we are going to hand out tonight resembles Gene in an uncanny way. Jane will be the first to notice, as well as Matt and Nedo who are on their way momentarily."

"Dave is here. From what I'm seeing right now, he's got his eye on Gene and is openly staring at him. I think I can smell the gears turning in that brain of his," said Eugenia, shaking her head.

"Oh God," sighed Dottie, "the tangled webs we weave."

"Well, let's go face the music." As they entered the dining area, Matt and Nedo showed up with Police Chief Chris in tow. Gene had his back to the men and therefore they didn't notice him at first, not until Matt sat across from him, next to his father. As Matt sat, he lifted his head to see who the new man was and froze in mid air.

"Oh my God," hissed Eugenia, "let's get this show on the road. I hope Jane waits to show that dumb ass picture."

Two men were now openly staring at Gene, making him feel uncomfortable and self- conscious.

"Ok, order, order," said Eugenia standing at the back of Gene's chair. "We're all going to introduce ourselves before we begin. We have several newbies here, so let's all get our tea and scones and goodies and settle in. We have a lot to cover tonight."

Claire, the local librarian, entered the room along with Seth, one of the local high school teachers. "Mom can't come tonight," said Claire, "she's feeling nasty. I have to report back to her."

Claire's mom was a noted psychic and witch. She was beloved by all who knew her in town. She and Father were good friends. They often found themselves at opposite ends of the spectrum, but both respected one another.

As they all settled in, Nedo took his seat next to Gene. Gene had gotten up and poured himself a cup of tea, added sugar and milk and sat down.

Nedo looked from Matt to Dave quizzically and then looked squarely at Gene as he sat down. Nedo looked back at Matt and then to Dave with a shocked look on his face.

Dave gave him a know-it-all grin that was bluntly interpreted as...*well Brian, what you gonna do now?*

Gene smiled a sheepish smile at him and Nedo nodded.

"Hi, I'm Brian," he said extending his hand.

"Eugene, but they all know me round here as Gene."

"Been here long?" Brian Nedo hissed.

"Yeah, bout six months, maybe a year now. I run the antique shop just down the road here."

"Where you from?" hissed Nedo.

"Alabama," came the friendly reply.

Nedo's face turned sheet white and he turned away to hide it. His stomach was in turmoil. "This is uncanny, this just can't be," he thought,

"Ok, we'll start with me and go round the room," said Eugenia when they were all settled.

"My name is Eugenia Simpkins and I'm from here in Emeryville."

"I'm Jane and my husband is Chris, the chief of police. We are both from Albany, New York."

"I'm Claire and I'm from here along with my mom, Katie. I am the local librarian."

"I'm Seth Collins and I'm a history teacher at the school."

"I'm Dave Bell and I'm from Shelbyville, Alabama."

Curiosity furrowed Gene's brow as he openly stared at Dave. Matt immediately picked up on it.

"I'm Matt Bell and I'm from Shelbyville, Alabama, Tomisina, Alabama and New York City."

Gene's eyes were almost bugging out of his head. His mouth was slightly open as he stared openly at Matt.

"I'm Father Munro, und you all know I come from God." Someone laughed and there were several giggles. "Naw, I'm originally from Scotland und then Saranac Lake, New York und then Albany und then here, with stretches here und there between," said Father.

"I'm Karen Bell and I'm from here in Emeryville."

"I'm Steve and I'm from Pepperell, Massachusetts and Albany, New York."

It was now Gene's turn. "Well," drawled Gene, "my name is Eugene Riley, but those of you who know me call me Gene. I'm from Tomisina, Alabama and Libertyville, Alabama and now from here in Emeryville." He was still staring at Matt.

"I'm Dottie, well…" and after a very long pause, "Dorothy Riley Bowmaker and I'm from Mobile, Alabama," she said in a quiet, hushed voice.

Dave shot out of his chair, a look of shock on his face.

"You're not related to David Bowmaker, are you?" he shouted.

"Unfortunately yes," said Dottie quietly. Dottie turned to Gene who looked like he was in a state of bewilderment and shock.

The room had turned deathly quiet as she asked Gene, in a voice that shook with emotion, "Your mother was Francine, am I right?"

Gene nodded his head yes.

Dottie started to cry. "You, sir, are my nephew. Francine was my sister," she said through her sobs.

"I thought you were dead," said Gene quietly.

"Funny you should say that," said Dottie, a note of resignation in her voice. "Yes, I'm supposed to be dead, but here I am."

"Bowmaker was the name of my lawyer," said Dave. He looked angry and upset. "The man, who if I'd not hired him, my daughter might still be alive and my son would not have to have grown up without a real father. Matt would never have been involved with Garrett Sellers."

Gene looked shocked. He said, slowly, "Garrett is the name of my twin brother. My identical twin brother."

~

[105]

All eyes turned toward Gene.

"Yes," said Dottie, "I recognized the boy in the picture. The one Eugenia showed me a few days ago."

She nodded to Gene to continue.

The room was deathly quiet as Gene said, "Ya see, my daddy was a mean and nasty son-of-a-bitch. When my mother divorced my father, she took me and my father…"

"Bradley," sneered Dottie, nodding again at Gene to continue.

"Well he took my brother Garrett. We never saw one another again."

Jane looked down at the picture she held in her hand. She frowned and said quietly, "I think you should see this Gene."

Gene held out his hand and took the picture. He stared at it a long time.

"That's me alright, at least a good likeness of me."

He looked questioningly at Dave and then Matt.

Dave said, "this man is wanted all across the south for murder. He's on a killing spree and anyone who gets in his way is dead. When is the last time you saw your brother?"

"I was about five or six. As I said, when he went with my pa, that was it. End of all communication. I remember the day so vividly, the day her and I, I mean Mom and I left. Garrett had a rabbit in one of his snares. Pretty little thing. He just killed it. Hit it over the head with a rock. I screamed and ran to Mom, who was standing in the back yard of our house. He followed me and called me a sissy and other names of course. Mom called him a bully and grabbed him and spanked him. He didn't cry, he just stood there and he told her one day he would kill her. Dad came out the back door and onto the porch and you know what he said to my ma, he said "yeah Francine, someday he and I will kill you both." That's the day we left. Grandpa took care of all the legal work, real simple, divorce, two kids, split them up."

"Ma died when I was about twenty or so," he continued. "She just disappeared one night, nothing was ever found of her. She is still a missing person down there. Gran and Pops held out until I was twenty-five. I sold the farm and went into the Navy. Got out and worked on oil rigs, but I still had this thought I wanted to be my own boss. I've always liked old things and I'm pretty good at fixing things up."

"I think we all need a breather," said Father Munro. "Let's refresh und relax for a moment while we digest all this information."

After a few minutes, Father looked at Gene quizzically and said, "What brought ya here Gene?"

"Well," said Gene, "I was just guided here. Intuition, something like that. I came into town and my inner voice told me this is it. I got a room from Mrs. Henshaw."

"The town busy body," said Eugenia with scorn in her voice.

Gene laughed, "Yes, I have learned to keep my mouth shut around her."

"Yes, you are going to have to keep quiet because this is a very real investigation," warned Chris.

"Matt here is a town policeman and this is Dave, he's FBI and so is Brian here."

"I'm surrounded," said Gene, sheepishly.

"We've come up with a dead end," said Nedo, "but one thing we are aware of, the murders are escalating. We have a good notion to believe that Matt here and maybe Dot, and now, especially you, are in real danger. He is headed this way and he means to kill Matt and we surmise anyone else associated with him."

Gene turned and eyed Nedo and then shaking his head sadly he said, "I believe you're right. I must tell you this so when I go off, so to speak, you are aware of what I'm going through. Just before he does something bad, Garrett, I mean, just before he has his killing sprees, I get severely depressed, almost suicidal. I get in these black moods with horrible nightmares and cold sweats. The last one was about three to four weeks ago. Visions of a small boy, screaming, running, dying. I never see the killer in any of the dreams."

"We're all here to help," said Father.

Nedo and the rest of the assembly nodded.

After lively discussions and a short business meeting, the group left a little before 10:00 pm. Nedo walked home with Dave, as he was staying with him.

Differently Double

Chapter Twenty-Seven

The next morning Katie listened with rapt attention to all that was being told to her by Dottie.

"Identical twins have connections that are just now being studied the way they should have been years ago," she said quietly. "Mind if I pay Mr. Riley a visit?"

"I don't think he'd mind, just don't beat around the bush. He's a sensitive but doesn't quite know what to do about it. This idea with being a twin to a very evil man isn't boding well with him," said Dottie.

"I think if Father and I visit him, we can give him some prayers and some spells for protection. I have a feeling he'll need it," said Katie.

The following day Katie walked to the rectory and met Father. Together they walked up the street toward Gene's. They noticed a black SUV in the small parking lot at the side of the shop.

~

"Och, I bet that's Nancy trying to strike up a deal again. She'll drive me nuts yet," muttered Father. "I made her the head of our Christmas auction und she's hitting up everyone in town und beyond for auction donations. It's our biggest fundraiser of the year. She's in charge of the auction, Carol is in charge of the soup und sandwiches und Karen is in charge of the desserts. Makes for a tidy package, or so I thought. I didn't realize that Nancy could be so exasperating sometimes, but I certainly don't know what I'd do without her. She is one of those unique people who comes along only once in a person's lifetime."

Katie smiled and nodded for Nancy was a dear friend, but she understood everything Father was saying. "I think once in a lifetime is all anyone could take," she retorted.

Father laughed and smiled.

After Nancy left, Gene made sure Mrs. Henshaw wasn't around. Her penchant for eavesdropping was legendary and he didn't want to take chances. He sat out three chairs near his counter and they all sat down. "I'll make tea," he said, but Father and Katie declined.

"What you have with your brother is called entanglement, for lack of a better word," said Father.

"It's a common metaphysical term und simply means that no matter how far apart you two are physically you still stay in touch with one another through an unseen bond. It's not apparent in all twins but enough of them, und in many cases, individuals without genetic connections also have it."

"Around here we all have a touch of it," said Katie. "It's a form of telecommunication."

Father continued, "We're not born evil, we grow into it, we embrace it und make it our own; just as one can make goodness und non-judgment their own."

Gene listened intently and said, "But when the dreams come, it's awful. The feelings, the hatred, the anger. I get so depressed afterwards."

Father nodded. "Yes, but you're aware when it's happening. We're going to give you some exercises und prayer und maybe, just maybe, we can make a difference. You have to remain in a state of mind where you can look at the visions of the killings und say *this is not mine* und push it away. I'm saying that this is a part of going into oneself, to see the vulnerability we all have, und all must suffer with. Alone time is not overrated, but time with others is also important. It's a balancing act."

So it was that during the ensuing weeks, Gene became fast friends with Father, Katie, Eugenia and his Aunt Dottie. They would often visit him and help him tend his small garden in back of the antique shop.

Chapter Twenty-Eight

Nedo sat back in the wicker chair and relaxed on this incredibly early morning. He was sitting on Dave's patio by his small garden. He scraped at some mulch with his toe and sighed. It was chilly and he wore a sweater.

"You're up early," said Dave, bringing his coffee to the chair next to Nedo's.

Nedo glanced at the woods behind the small apartment. "This is a very beautiful place," he commented. "Ever get the sensation that some people come here to hide?"

"Like Dottie?" said Dave with a knowing smile.

Nedo smiled and sighed as he nodded his head. "What do you propose we do with her?" he asked, looking directly at Dave.

Dave met his gaze, smiled and said, "at the moment, absolutely nothing."

"My thoughts exactly. I sure would like to know what happened, off the record of course, and where those two little girls are now, if they're still alive?"

"Knowing Bowmaker's underground, they could be anywhere. But, I'll tell you this, if he didn't kill 'em he made a buck on 'em to be sure," said Dave.

"There's so many women that end up in this situation, I just want to say, give 'em a chance, just another chance. But that's not the way it works sometimes. Hell, a lot of times. We're here to uphold the law. Is it fair? No. Is it just? No. Is it our duty? Yes. Where do you draw the line?"

Dave nodded his head and said, "I really want to talk to her. See what really happened. We could give her an opportunity to clear things up, but who knows what the state attorney for the prosecution will do. Remand her to jail? Bail? What?"

"She hasn't been formally charged. She's just a person of interest, far as I know," said Nedo.

He continued, "I know a few in that group will be questioning the situation, especially Chris. We better come clean. Maybe let a judge see her and all. She's not gonna want to leave and hell, if she runs again, we'll never find her."

"I don't think she'll run. She's tired of it all. I know it. She has too much to lose, especially here," said Dave.

~

Several days later, Dave and Nedo approached the tiny house at the end of Maiden Lane. They had done their homework and knew all the details of the case, including the fact that a fund had been set up many years ago to help with Dottie's defense.

Dottie had just come in from the barn and was sitting at the kitchen table catching up on her mail. She heard their footfalls on the back steps and hesitated when she saw who was visiting. She got up, opened the door on this quiet fall morning and ushered them in.

"Tea, coffee," she said. Both declined. "Sit," she ordered. "I think I know why you're here," she said, resignation in her voice.

"To be honest with you, we'd rather let this go, but I think if you bring this to the grave with you, you won't have peace," said Dave, quietly. "And it's our job."

"You're right. Looking over one's shoulders all the time isn't good. Makes for paranoia," she said in a quiet voice.

"You know of any lawyers down there you'd like to hire? Good defense attorneys. I know you could access the fund; it's still sitting in the bank and occasionally someone makes a deposit to it."

"What fund?" she questioned.

"The one many of the Mobile women started when you ran. You have a full-fledged defense fund in your name. And, it's intriguing that one person puts money into it yearly. This keeps it active at the bank it's in. Same person. We traced her and she lives in Indiana. Name's Sandy…"

Nedo was cut short by a gasp from Dotty who looked directly at him.

She raised her finger and said, "Elliot, Sandy Elliot. My husband's secretary and my part-time babysitter for the girls. Good God, she's got to be in her eighties by now."

"I think you should talk with Gene, as he's your closest relative. And talk to your attorney. See if they can find a good defense attorney for you in

Alabama and go from there. We're FBI, we can't get involved with the legal end, just the apprehension end. Got it?" said Dave.

"Dennis is my attorney," she said, shaking her head.

"Start with him. He can get the ball rolling on this. If they just want you for questioning without a formal warrant, maybe it'll work and we won't have to send you back down there right away. I strongly suggest he work with an attorney down there. The best defense you can find and buy. You have the money, use it. When this breaks it's gonna get media attention. A lot of media attention," said Nedo.

Several hours later the two men left the cozy kitchen. They were not feeling hungry as they walked to their car, for they had relented and had pie with ice cream and coffee, while Dottie told her entire story.

Differently Double

October

Chapter Twenty-Nine

Steve stood on the front sidewalk, looking at the large, red Victorian. Larry emerged from the front door, briefcase in hand. When he spotted Steve, he hesitated before he said, "no rest for the weary."

"Another case?" said Steve.

"Two, both natural causes I think. When I get there, I'll find out. What are you doing?" Larry inquired.

"Oh, getting ready to decorate for Halloween, my absolute favorite holiday," said Steve, an edge of amusement in his voice. "What kind of budget do we have for home decorating? Wait till you see my plans for Christmas!"

"No blowups, no fireworks, no loud music with screeching and moans and absolutely no six- foot spiders," said Larry with authority in his voice.

Steve frowned, "You're no fair" and went back to looking at the front of the house.

"Now I have acid indigestion," mumbled Larry as he got into his car.

Differently Double

Chapter Thirty

Lydia and Olivia were walking home from school. Olivia was going home with Lydia to study for an upcoming exam the following day, and to stay overnight.

"Ya know, it'll be Halloween in three weeks," commented Olivia. She was glancing up the street toward the house where Steve and Larry lived.

"Yup," said Lydia, giggling. "Steve's already at it, I mean decorating. My Grampa said it's a circus over there just listening to the two of them bicker about the Halloween decorations. Steve, I have a feeling, is the type of person who would go all-out. He says Halloween is his all- time favorite holiday."

"I believe it. He's nutty enough," said Olivia.

After several hours of intense studying, the two girls were called down to supper. The conversation centered around school and local goings-on around town. There was laughter and some teasing as Matt liked to tease the girls if he got the chance. After the dishes were cleaned up, the two girls decided that they had had enough of studying. They both felt comfortable with the material to be covered in the exam the following day.

They decided to take a walk toward the cemetery and back, and then early to bed so they would be fresh for the exam.

"Don't be too long," Karen told them, as they left the house.

They started out the driveway in the dusky stillness of early evening. They had managed to walk past the front of the old Victorian, where Larry and Steve lived, when they heard Larry bellow, "who in hell hands out fruitcakes for Halloween?"

Both girls stopped in the middle of the sidewalk, not wanting to miss one installment of the *Larry vs Steve Saga,* they waited. Spellbound.

Steve had just emerged from the open screen door that led to the front porch. He was smiling, almost laughing. "Now Larry, Larry, I think it's a grand idea," said Steve, halfway down the front steps of the porch. He had a sack of recyclables in his hand and was depositing them on the sidewalk for pick up the next day.

"For Christmas, it would be a good idea," shouted Larry, from the closed screen door. "Not Halloween. I know your fruitcakes are legendary, but…"

"I know," shouted Steve, his hand extended upward with one finger in the air and waving it around, "fruitcake cookies. That's a better idea than pumpkin cookies, which was my second choice."

Lydia and Olivia were standing on the sidewalk in the shadows of the two-hundred year old maple trees. Lydia said, "fruitcake, for Halloween? Fruitcake? You've got to be kidding."

"No," said Steve, approaching the two girls, a wide smile on his face. "I'm not kidding at all. Do you know my fruit is brining at this very moment in four liters of the best brandy money can buy."

"No one would eat fruitcake unless they were drunk anyway," sneered Olivia.

"Not. My fruitcake is very famous. It's delectable with a hint of ginger, nutmeg and molasses and all that delicious candied fruit and walnuts. Yes! And then the bake and the cooling and the rum rub, followed by a powdered sugar dump and a cheese cloth wrap. And then another rum rub in one week, followed by one more powdered sugar dump and another rum rub. Oh my. My taste buds are starting to salivate," Steve said breathlessly.

Olivia rolled her eyes. "Fruitcake?" she muttered.

"I like the idea of the pumpkin cookies," said Lydia sheepishly. She was still staring at Steve, her mouth slightly ajar.

Larry came onto the porch and just looked at the three of them. "This is one for the books," he muttered.

Living with Steve was a never ending journey; an event. Most of the time he didn't know if he was joking, leading you on or serious. You just had to wait and see which way the wind blew.

Steve's face was now a nice shade of puce. His beloved fruitcakes were being assaulted and he didn't like it one bit.

"Did you know that on All Hallow's Eve, in Ireland, an Irish version of fruitcake called barmbrack is served," he said haughtily.

"We, ah have to go now," said Olivia. They turned abruptly and made a hasty retreat.

Larry, joining Steve on the sidewalk, put his hands on his hips and said, "now you've done it. Fruitcakes will be the talk of the town tomorrow and well into next week."

Steve just shrugged his shoulders, a broad smile lighting up his face.

"So," said Steve, turning to face Larry, "I think if I put Halloween costumes on my collection of pink lawn flamingos and place them at strategic places on the lawn, it will be a nice statement for Halloween!"

Larry thought he was going to cry. "Let's go and have a drink and we'll discuss this," he said.

They locked arms and headed for the local tavern for beers.

"Do you remember David Obb?" said Steve. Both men were perched on stools at the bar of the local tavern.

"Usual?" asked Artie, the local tavern keeper.

"Yup. Hey, wait a minute. I've heard the hard root beer is really, really good," said Steve.

"Want some?" asked Artie.

"Yeah, I like root beer," said Steve

"This is different, you know it's alcohol," said Artie, brusquely.

"Had any of it?" asked Steve.

"Yeah, I kinda like it, nice change. Better than the peach one."

"I think we both should have a bottle," said Larry. "I'm game to try anything different."

"Something different?" asked Artie. "You should try the concoction that Claire had the other night at the library meeting. Took me three tries to get up from my seat, and I usually don't drink."

"Oh," said Steve, "do tell. I'm always interested in new things."

"Somehow, some bastard put my name in for the library board. So, being as community minded as I am," said Artie, sarcastically, "I, of course, went to a library board meeting. Claire had some there. Brought it in as a joke. The teetotalers on the board had some too. It was a merry time getting the older ones out of that meeting. Old lady Bouchert, tipsy? Now, there's a sight," he chuckled.

Steve started to laugh.

"Anyway," he continued, "there's this bourbon, and it's mixed with cream. Ya know, like the Irish Cream, only this is bourbon. Ok, so you take Bourbon Cream and add root beer and vanilla ice cream. I had three and was so incoherent by the time I left the meeting I could've voted on anything. I mean, this went down like syrup; real smooth. You don't realize you're smashed until you go to stand up."

Larry rolled his eyes and smiled, visions of merriment at the library board meeting danced in his head.

Steve looked at him and wondered just what he was thinking.

Both men shook their heads and turned back to their frosty glasses of root beer.

"David Obb, David. Psi Kappa Py? Big guy, know it all," said Larry taking a swallow of his root beer. "Whoa, this gives root beer a whole new meaning. I could get used to this. I like this, Artie."

Artie just nodded and smiled.

"The diva man we called him," said Steve.

"Third year of college?" asked Larry, now conjuring up the guys identity in his brain.

"Yeah, him," said Steve. "Remember the skinny dipping party we had and they stole all his clothing and left him a blue dress two sizes too small for him? He had to walk all the way into town to the dorm. When he came in, he blamed me and literally tore up the place to get to me?"

"Yessss," said Larry hesitantly.

"Well, I just want to confess that it was indeed all my fault, all my idea and I am sooo glad I did it," Steve said gleefully.

"Why are you telling me this now?" said Larry.

"I don't know, just reminiscing I guess," said Steve reflectively. "Hey Artie, can I have some of your famous stuffed mushrooms?"

Artie nodded his head and headed for the kitchen, which was right off the bar.

Chapter Thirty-One

It was a bright, sunny morning and it was early. The phone rang at Dottie's house. She picked it up and began her greeting, "Good morning, Daylily...

"Get over here now!" shouted a high-pitched, angry voice.

"Who the hell is this?" she said, getting agitated.

"You know who it is. Just get those damned horses off my front lawn," screamed Steve.

She heard the click of the phone and then dead air space.

She furtively looked out the window of her kitchen toward the paddock and her heart sank. No Ferd and no Valerie. "Shit, shit, shit," she said as she ran out the door and up the street toward Steve and Larry's house.

As she passed the cafe, Suzie ran out and shouted, "the gang gave them donuts and then they were on their way. Looked like they were on a mission."

"Mission my ass," cursed Dottie to herself. She gripped the lead rope she managed to grab on the way out her back door. Years of experience conditioned her to the fact that when you owned horses you always had a lead rope somewhere in your house where you could grab it easily.

She ran past the Health Center and slowed down as she approached Lydia's house. Passing the house Lydia's mom opened the front door and called out to her, "just called you. I heard Steve bellow from here."

Dottie rolled her eyes. She was almost in tears. Somehow Valerie seemed to admire Steve. She couldn't stay away. Whenever she managed to escape, she would take Ferd with her and they ended up in Steve and Larry's yard. Whenever Dottie led a trail ride out toward the cemetery, Valerie, with her plump rear end, always managed a little dance as they passed Steve's house. She would nicker and snort as if she wanted Steve to hear her.

There they were; the both of them, thoroughly ensconced on the front lawn. They were careful not to touch the pink, plastic flamingos that occasionally dotted the premises here and there, but the Halloween costumes that were on them were scattered over all parts of the lawn. Valerie, her thick dappled grey and white neck sported a pair of lime green pants from a Ninja Turtles costume. She had a witches hat hanging from her mouth. Ferd looked like a rockstar with a purple wig cocked nattily on one side of his head. He was shaking it, but the buckle on his halter had hooked on the bottom of the long tresses and it was firmly in place.

Steve was cowering behind the front screen door and now he came out onto the porch. She could clearly hear gales of laughter coming from Larry who was just inside the door.

Larry managed to say, "looks like we're going to have a tea party," and then burst into another round of laughter.

"Really," said Steve, "this is…"

He was interrupted when Valerie placed one foot on the front porch step and looked up at him with large, liquid brown, soulful eyes. She was in love, in love with Steve.

Dottie, grabbing her halter, clicked the lead rope on and managed to back her up and turn her around.

"She somehow has managed to fall in love with you," she said curtly.

Steve just stood there dumbfounded. "What?" he said in a hoarse whisper.

"Have you ever noticed how she acts whenever she sees you, hears your voice, passes your house? She's smitten."

Larry, hearing this doubled over in laughter yet again.

"I don't have the heart to sell her, so get over it," Dottie snapped. She removed the hat from Valerie's jaws and took the lime green pants from across her back and threw them on the step.

"Ferd," she yelled. "Home, NOW."

Ferd turned and began trotting toward home, the purple wig he sported flopping in the breeze. As Ferd passed the Cafe, a crowd had assembled and they applauded as he passed. He did his best to slow a little and show off some of his high-step trot but a bellow from Dottie, who was halfway up the block, released him from his moment of reverie. He reluctantly headed for home at a full gallop.

Differently Double

Chapter Thirty-Two

It was a chilly Friday night, but no rain was forecast and fortunately not two feet of snow either. Halloween was in full swing. There usually was an overabundance of kids roaming the streets, as local farm families would bring their children and their friends into town by the pickup truck load. The Village Board set hours for trick-or-treating from five thirty to eight pm. In the past, roving gangs of kids would disrupt the quiet of the village in the wee hours of the morning and the next day the village maintenance crew had their jobs cut out for them. Shattered pumpkins, toilet paper, shaving cream, wax and the occasional small vehicle gingerly placed on someone's roof. Once, some students had filled a teacher's car with popped popcorn. Now, with extra police patrols, Halloween had tamed down somewhat.

Steve sat on his porch in a ghost outfit, made from an old sheet. He was so quiet and still in his chair that he scared most of the trick-or-treaters when he moved to give them one of his treats; his fruit cake cookies. They were really, really good, according to most of the kids who dared eat them.

Larry handed out Snickers bars.

Differently Double

November

Chapter Thirty-Three

He stayed fit and trim. He moved around a lot and got odd jobs so he didn't have to socialize much. He was on the move, having found a Mathew Bell and a Dave Bell involved in a case last year in central New York. What a coincidence. It had to be them.

He had stayed in Tennessee for a few weeks and found a job as a busboy and waiter at a local roadhouse. A real dive, but busy. It had its curious selection of prowling waitresses, most of which he just couldn't deal with.

Now he was going to have to leave. Why didn't that waitress just leave him alone? Why did she want more out of him than he was willing to give? She trailed him to his motel room and demanded he let her in. He didn't.

The following day she followed him to the park during his lunch break. That was the last straw. He hid her body among the rocks on a cliff.

He showed up for work the next day and was asked where she was. He looked from one to another of his co-workers and shook his head. Dammed if I know he told them. The next day, he was on his way again, headed north toward New York.

~

November in upstate New York was a combination of dreary, foggy, brisk cold days interspersed with warm, sunny days. An occasional burst of snow or sleet sometimes made an appearance at the end of the month.

It was time for Eugenia to put up all her bird feeders; all twelve of them. She would drive to Howard's to pick up one-hundred pounds of cracked corn and four-hundred pounds of black oil sunflower seeds. Howard grew both and was glad to supply the locals so they could feed the *birdies*. Next, Eugenia would visit the local hardware store and purchase two cases of suet and one-hundred pounds of a peanut and millet seed blend. She was proud to shop locally.

Eugenia had the most birds over winter than anyone else in the town and she was a regular contributor to the Bird Count put on by Cornell University each year.

"Why don't you just let me deliver it?" asked Howard.

"Nope," said Eugenia, "I keep two-hundred pounds of it in the car for ballast. Besides, if I get stuck on the ice, I spread sunflower seeds. Better than that salt stuff they put on the roads."

"Ahhh," said Howard, "I've noticed lots of sunflowers growing in the ditches lately. How many times you get stuck last winter?"

"None of your damn business," came the terse reply

Matt stood on Eugenia's porch. They were bundled up for the cold but, by the time they were finished, he knew they would be un-bundled. Lydia stood on the ladder, hooking in one pole that held two bird feeders and a suet cage. Matt put in brackets with lag screws, the same ones he had removed several months previously.

"Look what I have here," beamed Eugenia, showing off yet another new bird feeder. She was dressed in a pink hat with turquoise earmuffs and yellow gloves and a coat that looked like it came from the seventies and beyond. It was a mauve pink color and made of some sort of material that looked like quilted satin. It was the ugliest coat Matt had ever seen. He had dubbed the coat the *Space Cadet-Coat*.

He remembered the day she bought it. Eugenia, Dottie, Nancy, Ellen, and his wife had gone to Albany and visited the local Salvation Army Thrift Store. Eugenia had picked out the coat; on sale for just three dollars. His wife had come back from the shopping trip exasperated. She told him she didn't know where her mother's taste in fashion came from, but it sure wasn't her.

"She told us it would be her barn coat," Karen exclaimed, "and Dottie told her NOT in her barn."

Eyeing Matt looking at her Eugenia said "My birdie coat. I wear it to help Dottie in the barn, feed the birds and go walking. It's really warm, but I do look a fright, don't I? I'd miss this coat if anything ever happened to it," she continued.

"That's why I haven't washed it yet and besides, I want to be buried in this coat."

Matt looked at her, turned and muttered, "If you took it off it would probably stand up and walk by itself."

"I heard that Matthew," she said, sternly.

They finished the feeders. Already birds were congregating to check out the buffet.

They went inside where the little wood stove in the corner of the kitchen was blazing. Matt and Lydia brought in more wood to fill the woodbox, while a pot of tea and fresh biscuits sat on the table along with honey and homemade jam.

Differently Double

Chapter Thirty-Four

It was sunny and unseasonably warm for November. Dottie had put several horses out in the pasture and decided to retire to her kitchen for a brief cup of tea between lessons. Several riders were putting their horses through their paces. Valerie and some of her cohorts were in the paddock when a car pulled up in front of the stable. Dottie heard the door shut and then she heard footsteps on her back porch.

Looking out the kitchen window she saw Steve with Larry right behind him. Steve was holding a bag of carrots. As she opened the door Steve said sheepishly, "This is for my valentine."

Dottie couldn't help but notice Larry, trying to suppress his laughter as he stood behind Steve. "I'm deathly afraid of horses," Steve said furtively, "so don't ask me to go out and feed her."

"I think if you did, she'd want to climb in bed with you tonight," muttered Dottie. Larry was losing composure fast and almost fell off the porch backward.

Eugenia appeared around the corner and spied Steve. Steve looked dejected, but Larry was having a good ol' time.

"First date?" she said as she approached the porch and spied the bag of carrots.

Larry now totally lost it. He was doubled over with laughter, tears streaming from his eyes.

"Not funny," wailed Steve. "Why me?"

"Why not?" said Eugenia. "Friendships with animals that have bonded over many lifetimes are still valid in this lifetime."

Steve's face was like a mask. "You think so?" he squeaked.

"I do," said Dottie. "There is something there, don't know what, but something."

"Come on, let's go see. Don't worry she won't attack you, just remember she weighs about nine hundred pounds."

"And she has teeth," muttered Steve.

Valerie had her head hung over the top rail of the fence, anticipation in her eyes. She was grunting and snorting as the group approached.

[133]

"That's her *look who's visiting pose*," sighed Dottie. "It's bad enough I have several students that need attention and now I have a lovesick mare." Dottie scratched Valerie under her chin, but it was obvious that she only had eyes for Steve. She reached out with her muzzle and with quivering lips she managed to place a large, wet, sloppy kiss right in the middle of Steve's chest. Steve was frozen to the spot.

"Here, give her that carrot," said Dottie. "Hand flat, carrot on top."

Steve reluctantly extended his hand and the velvet lips tickled his palm as Valerie took the carrot gingerly. Other horses were gathering for their fair share. When one approached Steve a little too close, Valerie flattened her ears and chased the intruder away.

"She's jealous! Oh my God, a jealous woman," shrieked Larry.

Steve managed to pat Valerie's cheek and look into her big, brown eyes. They were intelligent. He started mumbling to her. She cocked her head as if she understood every word and utterance from him.

Steve spent the rest of the afternoon getting acquainted with the horses, and always, Valerie was at his side. She had managed to shove Larry out of the way and get between him and Steve. Larry, somewhat used to horses, patted her neck and he too found a fondness for her in his heart.

Differently Double

Chapter Thirty-Five

Gene's nightmares were a little less violent now and bordered more on panic and anticipation. Dark shadows haunted his dreams, but whenever the madness started, Gene would use some of the techniques and prayers Father had given him. He talked to Dottie, Katie, and Eugenia frequently about the situation. One day a thought occurred to him. What if those dark shadows were what drove Garret to kill? What if he was seeing and feeling exactly what his brother felt and saw as his brother was about to murder his victims?

Gene immediately started a diary, writing down everything that he dreamed; all his feelings and the times and the dates. He was relentless with it. Sometimes in his dreams, there were flashes of street signs, motel marquees and parking lots. He never saw a man, just shadows, but he wrote down everything.

Several days later, Eugenia saw what he was doing.

"Hum," she said, "I wonder if this would be any good to the police?"

"I think they would lock me up as loony," said Gene.

"I don't think so. Here's the name of a street and the name of a motel. I wonder if it would be good at tracking him?"

Gene shrugged and shook his head. "I'll go see Matt and Dave," he said.

~

Gene had shared his *Dream Book*, as he called it, with Dave and Matt the next day. They immediately transferred the information from the book into proper channels.

Three days later a local jogger in a city park on the outskirts of Nashville, Tennessee found the remains of a corpse stuffed unceremoniously into the crevice of a cliff. It was determined that the middle-aged waitress from a local truck stop was bludgeoned to death with a blunt object. After interviewing witnesses, the police determined that it was indeed the work of Garrett, who was one of her co-workers. He had stayed at the motel that Gene clearly saw in one of his nightmares and had written the name of it down in his book.

The more Gene thought about the dreams and the coincidences, the more memories he uncovered. Some were nice and others bordered on insanity. Then he suddenly remembered that when he was in the service, nightmares plagued him there also, but not as frequently. He remembered seeing an army shrink. The doctor's name was Robert Menzies and he was one of the professors at the grad school near the base. Menzies counseled a lot of military personnel. He and Gene had become fast friends. Gene, along with others, had been the subject of a study about identical twins and their co-dependence on one another. But the years rolled away and by the time Gene was out of the service and a deckhand on an oil rig, he had lost track of the man. Gene made a mental note to look him up.

In the last week of November, Dr. Menzies, a short, aged, weathered man, full of cynicism and the attitude of one who has seen it all, decided to visit Gene. Much to Menzies' chagrin, he arrived in town just as the Christmas season was beginning. After all, he was a devout agnostic.

Chapter Thirty-Six

Steve came into the antique shop a little harried and on a mission. His glasses steamed as he entered the warm confines of the shop which was heated by a wood stove. It was cold and the snow blew across the road in little fingers leaving Gene with the hourly duty of sweeping and shoveling out the parking lot.

He nodded to Gene and said, "Have any old Santa's? Remember the old ones, not the blow-up kind, but the ones about three feet high with a light bulb in the base?" inquired Steve. "They were made of heavy plastic."

"Yeah," said Gene. "I have several in the barn. If you want, I'll have them out for you tomorrow. I think I have a snowman and a Mary, Joseph, and Jesus too."

"Oh, that sounds great," said Steve, rubbing his hands together in anticipation. "I hate blow-ups. Reminds me of the kinky, blow-up dolls you see in the porn stores."

Gene looked at him and started to laugh. "Been there, done that," he muttered.

Differently Double

December

Chapter Thirty-Seven

It was the first Saturday in December and Christmas light decorating had begun. This year, the village board was hoping to take the prize away from their neighboring rival ten miles away. The annual light displays had always been a fun way for the local villages and towns within the county to have a friendly contest as to who had the best lighting displays. The lights increased tourism in the area as many folks from surrounding counties and even some of the larger cities made their way to these small towns and villages for a ride. Weekend evenings were the most crowded. The local papers provided maps and directions of all the area light displays. Television and radio news broadcasts had daily updates on the progress of the contest. Shops also stayed open later so locals could shop without encountering the madness and crowds of the large malls in the cities.

Dave stood in the driveway of his apartment, ready at a moment's notice to start stringing Christmas lights. Larry and Steve stood on the front lawn conversing on final lighting plans. A light blanket of snow covered the lawn and trees.

"I like the idea of blue and white next year," sighed Steve. "Multi is so tacky and white is just dull and boring."

"Next year it will be yellow," Larry muttered.

Dave was not going to get into this conversation. No way!

"Ok ok," said Steve, "but promise me next year we can have blue and white...promise?"

Larry just hung his head and Dave had all he could do to suppress a laugh.

"Just what are you doing with a carload of plastic lawn ornaments?" inquired Larry. He said this to Steve with a great deal of apprehension.

"Now," said Steve, "you can have your multi's and I can have my lawn ornaments. Do you see that spot way over there in the trees? Well, what a nice place to put the Holy family. It's off to the side and, more importantly, in a place that will be away from the lights and glitter of the main house. It will be secluded and natural so people will see it because it'll be lit but in the dark of the trees, and away from everything else."

"Makes sense," said Larry, "What about the snowman, the Santa and sled?"

"We can put them on the roof or the lawn in front," said Steve.

"I'm afraid of the wind we get here in the last weeks of the year, so I vote the lawn," said Larry.

"Very welcoming," said Steve thoughtfully.

"That snowman is kinda cute, what about over near the manger scene. Ya know, cold, northern winter and all. He could just stand there next to the manger. Maybe a little way off," injected Dave, meekly.

"Nice idea," said Steve. "Let's see how it looks. We could always put him near the sidewalk or maybe in front of your door," alluding to the front door of Dave's apartment in the carriage house, "if that doesn't work."

"Should've been a designer," muttered Dave.

~

With holiday preparations well underway, Gene was also caught up in the celebratory mood. He decorated his shop and even put a star high up in one of the trees near his driveway. Mrs. Henshaw commented to many of her friends that the star had to be over one-hundred feet in the air and how on earth did he get it up there. He certainly didn't climb that tree, or did he?

Gene smugly smiled to himself as he had his good friend, Tom at the junkyard, come over with his bucket crane and connect it up for him. Tom also had Alex go over with the bucket and put the Santa and reindeer light display on the tallest of Howard's silos.

Chapter Thirty-Eight

Nathan parked the big rig in front of the café. He needed coffee and he needed it bad. Jumping out, he almost ran into Matt, who was walking down the sidewalk with his partner Joe. "Sorry," he yelled as he yanked open the door to the café.

"Hey Nathan," yelled Suzie, over the din. "Coffee to go?"

He nodded.

Matt joined him in line. "Ya look like you're in a hurry," he said.

"Yeah, just hired on a bunch of really wise asses and I gotta get back and make sure no one dies. I can just see it now, chain saw jousting or something stupid like that. This is going to be a nightmare, I can tell."

Matt looked at him quizzically.

"My company's got the contract for the State Lands up on the side of West Mountain. Twenty-five-hundred acres, lot of work, lot of wood, lot of headaches and the State has marked the trees it wants out and the ones that stay. There are two-hundred-year-old cherries up there and a lot of spruce and pine. I needed to hire more crews, so I got some new guys. See how they work out. I'm housing them at the ol' Clinton Place. My dad owns the place now. House has decent water and electricity and all. Just a dump though. I'm sure you'll be seeing them around with us. The usual migrants who hire on for several months and then they're on their way."

"Well," he said, "got to get back. At least all of them are good with chain saws. I don't have to train any of them and they won't kill themselves or anyone else. At least I hope not," said Nathan as he headed for his truck with his coffee. He started it and roared off in the direction of the woods, the large log handler swinging gracefully on the rear of the eighteen-wheeler.

Differently Double

Chapter Thirty-Nine

December twenty-first would soon be here and with it the annual bonfire and solstice ceremony. Hosted by Dottie and Eugenia's group and the firemen's auxiliary, it was an anticipated event. The days would be getting longer after this night until the longest day and the shortest night would coincide in summer solstice on June twenty-first. The *die-hard* Christians dubbed it the *Waiting for the Light* ceremony, alluding to Christmas just four days away, and also attended the event in droves.

Several days before the annual bonfire a large bucket loader would appear on the grounds of the local conservation camp. Hemmed in between two mountains, it afforded a peaceful place for such an event. The loader would scrape away all vestiges of snow and ice. Wooden planks, stuck into upright concrete blocks would serve as benches and several loads of logs and firewood would be dumped near the site.

Regardless of the meaning, all who showed up eagerly waited for the fire to start and the mulled cider, coffee, tea, and hot chocolate to be served. Hot chili was served in bowls as well as hamburgers and hotdogs. The firemen sold the food and the money went toward needed equipment. You brought your mugs and the fill-ups were free, served under a canopy replete with a propane heater. Alcohol was allowed, but it was bring your own, and there was a lot of supervision by the locals.

Snowmobiles were parked beside cars. Cross country skis and snowshoes stood upright, their tails stuck in the banks of snow that surrounded the large plowed area, several acres in size. Pastor Teresa said a bonfire blessing and Father also said a prayer and the celebration was on.

Old fears, as well as wishes for the coming year, were written on paper. The paper was carefully folded and, at the right time, were thrown into the fire. As the smoke rose and ashes drifted upward on the gentle breeze on this dark evening before moonrise, the wishes and hopes of all those participating were carried into the starry heavens. Spirits were high and everyone joked and talked or sang songs.

Snowmobile suits and large woolen parkas were the manner of dress for most, with fleece and fur-lined hats and gloves a necessity. The Methodist Church and the local bank had a huge box at the site near the refreshment tent where one could donate unused mittens, socks, hats and underwear for local children and families in need. The school found that most children had hats and gloves but many children from poorer families in the area had no socks, and for many, no underwear. A majority of the donations consisted of packages of Hanes or Fruit of the Loom. It was thoroughly stressed that underwear and socks be *new*. People also knitted and crocheted scarves and mittens for the occasion and were more than happy to donate.

As the light from the fire illuminated the valley floor, the dark vestiges of East and West Mountains surrounded the gathering. The sky was ablaze with stars. The yips and howls from one of the packs of local coyotes could be heard occasionally in the distance. It was cold tonight, a balmy ten degrees shouted Marty, the fire chief, over his megaphone. People shouted their blessings and there seemed to be no inhibitions as the bonfire blazed and illuminated faces of people and animals milling about in cheerful and contemplative moods.

Merry Christmas and Happy Solstice were heard many times. Lydia loved wishing all a happy solstice, for with this came the hope of spring and summer and the end of dreadful winter. She had to bundle up with ten pounds of clothing just to go to school, which took her another ten minutes just to get ready in the morning. She hated being late, but no matter how hard she tried, she was late most of the time.

Eugenia, sheltering her mug of hot chocolate in her hands, muttered to Dottie "did you know that when I went into the Mini Mart the other day to go to the bathroom, I had so many clothes on I couldn't get my hand around to wipe myself."

"Did I have to know that?" sneered Dottie, "I mean really?"

"Well it's the truth, I hate winter for only one thing...the clothing. Ice and snow I can take but the clothing? Hell, you need seven layers just to step out the damn door to get the mail."

"Wait till January," said Dottie, "when all the water pipes in the barn start to freeze and I'm dealing with heat tapes everywhere and a monstrous heat bill. And then people are calling up saying I'll freeze if I have my lesson today or will you take care of my horse today as I can't get the car started."

"All they have to do is put on long underwear. You know the kind that's supposed to wick the water away. The under something," said Eugenia reflectively.

"Oh, that stuff," retorted Dottie. "Tried it. It was like wrapping duct tape around a marshmallow."

"Well, there's a ray of sunlight in all of this," said Eugenia, reflectively, "I got my first seed catalog in the mail yesterday."

Differently Double

Chapter Forty

"Ya know," Menzies remarked to Father quite casually, "I have a lot of papers written about Gene's condition. He's a study in mental anguish and why evil parents should be sterilized."

"Matter of opinion," said Father quietly. "Your description of evil und mine are two different things."

"Yup, that's what makes this so interesting," said Menzies, "just our discussions and the need to be opposite makes for a great time. I mean, I learn something about your thinking and you learn something about mine."

Father laughed as usual. They had become great friends over the past few weeks and they enjoyed an occasional breakfast and time together.

"You, an agnostic, und me a Catholic priest," Father said as he shook his head in amazement. He did this each time he thought of it.

"My parish secretary still can't get over the number of crazies I hang with," said Father reflectively.

"Let's face it, Gene is pretty passive and easy going, but I have seen another side to him, a dark side. A side he tries to suppress," said Menzies.

"But, instead of suppressing, we should be trying to take the evil from him und teach him that when it comes, it's not welcome," countered Father. "Pure evil is the transmutation of our souls. The listening to the other side of you, the not-so-good side, the side that no one wants to face. Evil drives us to be good in many cases; in others, it has just the opposite effect. How would we know good, if it isn't evil; black if there isn't white? It is how we treat these idealisms that are the core of one's life..."

"True," said Menzies, "but I find that under hypnosis many people find a side of themselves they don't like, but they still have to address it at some point in their lives. What is it that Blaise Pascal once said? Oh yes, All of humanity's problems stem from man's inability to sit quietly in a room alone."

"But fear," continued Father, "when one's mind is not free, those inhibitions cloud your judgment, your experience, your opinions und they keep you chained to them. These are the people who cannot stand on their own. The drugs, alcohol, religious und community intolerance that all play into the fear business. The inability to go within und see yourself as you are. When your mind is free, free of hate, jealousy und fear, you are free to go out und explore with an open mind. We make life too complicated. God is simple," said Father. "Why do we need an interpreter to interpret God? God should sing within our hearts at all times, but we look elsewhere for God. Some find God early in life, some later und some not at all. I would be out of a job if everyone could interpret God in his or her way und live by it. But it's not the case," he said sadly.

"Oh, all that spiritual hocus pocus, but you have some valid points," laughed Menzies. "I love when we agree to disagree."

Chapter Forty-One

Lydia was busy helping her mom decorate the tree and baking cookies. The outside of the house was decorated before the tree, so they, like many of the neighbors, could participate in the lighting event which started the first week in December. The judging was held on the twenty-first with an article about the winners in the local paper.

One of the neighboring villages had a life-size nativity in their town square, eclipsing many of the lighting displays in the area. Emeryville had a train and a Santa village in their town square near the Health Center and another lighting display near the Town Garage. One of the town employees took the large loader, which was not used in winter, and pulled it out front and decorated the entire machine in thousands of blinking lights. He even had a Santa sitting on the seat.

"I think for next year we need a real carousel, all decorated and running for all the kids," remarked Lydia as she removed a pan of gingerbread from the oven.

"It would be a cold ride," remarked Karen.

"Yeah, but look at all the fun and all that hot chocolate."

"Sounds like a great idea for next year," said Karen. "Speaking of hot chocolate, let's have some."

~

Hundreds of cars flocked to the tiny villages and towns in this central New York Region to view the lights, do some shopping at many of the unique shops, eat at local restaurants and cafés and generally have a festive time. Holiday cheer abounded everywhere.

Olivia's concert was on the eighteenth. Lydia and her Mom attended, along with Eugenia and Katie.

Phoning her mother the day of the concert, Karen innocently asked: "You're not going in that coat, are you?"

"No, that's my birdie coat," said Eugenia "not good enough for the school."

"Thank you, thank you, thank you," yelled Karen as she hung up the phone. "I just don't have the heart to leave her in the balcony."

~

"What ya doin? asked Olivia casually. She was peeking over her brother's shoulder as he held an oxy-acetylene welding torch at the ready. They were in the garage of their home, the door open to the very chilly afternoon.

"I'm getting back at that Alex, that's what," he answered.

She noticed the nice new torque wrench and then she noticed he was welding a steel box around the wrench.

"It'll take him months to open this," he gleefully said.

She noticed the wrapping paper and flocked ribbon at the ready for when the project was finished and cooled from the heat. He would wrap it all up for his friend with nice, colorful paper and a tidy bow.

"Ya see, last year he gave me this great tire gauge. The problem is he wrapped it in twenty rolls of duct tape first and then bolted a steel frame around it. He wrapped it up all nice and pretty and hands it to me with this stupid grin on his face. I'm just getting even with him this year."

"I heard he gave Tom some shirts, but the box was huge," Olivia said. "They were inside of twelve boxes, all wrapped up inside of one another. Tom was furious when he finally got to the shirts, but he did laugh."

Chapter Forty-Two

Despite all the holiday preparations, life still continued amongst all the hustle and bustle of this festive season. Howard and countless other farmers still had to milk all their cows. The goat farm still had to produce its cheese, local retailers and many of their employees were working overtime and the local logging company, with its crew of loggers, was still in the woods at 7:00 am each morning.

~

Lydia's family usually attended Mass on Christmas Eve, leaving plenty of time for presents, meals and visiting on Christmas Day. Matt's foster father, Richard Young, and his wife, Gloria, visited every Christmas Day from New York City. Karen and Eugenia cooked a large meal and all had a great time. As they were getting older and Gloria walked with a cane, the visits were usually short and were accompanied by Gloria's comments about Richard being too cheap to rent a hotel room for the night. Karen always remarked about them staying at their house in the small guest bedroom, but Richard wouldn't hear of it. Somehow, he didn't like being away from his home, even though it was three and a half hours from Emeryville to the city.

As the school was dismissed two days before the holiday and wasn't in session the week between Christmas and New Year, many of the kids got together during the holidays. Others visited relatives for a day or so and several made ski trips with their families.

The Fish and Game Pond was open for ice skating and many enjoyed the nightly bonfires and skating. Hot dogs, sandwiches and snacks were served in the clubhouse and several of the old-timers assembled for a nightly game of cards. The snowshoeing trails were open to the public as were the snowmobile trails. Many took advantage of the activities.

~

After the business of Christmas Day and all the Mass preparations and services, Father's life was finally settling down this Friday after Christmas Day. The bowl games would be in full swing for the next week. He was out to dinner every night and it was a grand time of year. A grand time indeed!

[153]

Father had spoken to his brother in Ayer, Scotland and had talked to nephews and nieces, many of them living in Ireland and several in France. He found all of them in good health and happiness.

He had said goodbye to his new-found friend Dr. Menzies, as Menzies also had holiday engagements. The good doctor had not packed enough clothing for this part of the world and the night of the solstice bonfire, he almost froze to death even though people had lent him plenty of warm clothing and heavy boots and socks. This brought on a cold and he was still sniffling when he left. He told Father he was not visiting again until it was at least eighty degrees. Father just laughed and said he would be in touch with new developments.

~

Gene was a guest at several Christmas and after-Christmas meals and was having the time of his life. But, the troubling sleep and dreams were still plaguing him. Dottie and Father had told him to sit on the side of the bed at night and ask the angels and spirits to not send him out that night. They explained that many times during sleep one moves into a mode of sleep where the spirit goes out of the body. While the physical body is recharging for the night, the etheric body and the mind is alive and charging by other methods. Sometimes it is visiting people in distress or assisting in other trials and tribulations, and sometimes it gets an education from etheric realms. Either way, when one wakes one does not remember, but the lasting effect of all this activity was exhaustion.

The method lasted until one night he forgot to do it. That night he dreamed he was inside of a castle, somewhere in Europe, proceeding up a very narrow, winding, claustrophobic set of stairs. When he got to a certain space he would look into a room and there was a banquet going on. The people would motion for him to come and join them, but they seemed to be on the next floor down and when he stepped out of the doorway there were no stairs to get down to them. So, he kept climbing. Occasionally he would hear occasional screams of one in distress and see a shadowy figure veiled in darkness.

"What does it all mean?" he mused. "What does it all mean?"

~

"What did you get for Christmas?" asked Lydia. She was sitting on a chair in Eugenia's kitchen table munching on a granola and oatmeal cookie.

"Well, I got another wind chime for my collection. The problem is instead of doing my puzzle last evening I managed to untangle the mess this friend of mine made when she got it out of the box to look at it. She couldn't get it back in so she wrapped it up halfway in and halfway out of the box." Eugenia smiled thoughtfully.

"Oh?" said Lydia, quizzically. "Now, let me guess. It's from Nancy?"

Her grandmother gave her a knowing smile and continued.

"She ordered four of them. One for me, one for Dottie, one for her and one for the auction at the church. The one she couldn't get back into the box she gave to me."

"Ohhhhh," said Lydia, now thoroughly confused. "How thoughtful...Why didn't she just keep that one for herself?"

"With her, it doesn't work that way. She gave it to me for Christmas because she knows I'll fix it and appreciate it. That's what you just banged into with your head when you put that napkin in the wastebasket."

Lydia glanced at the area and saw the large hummingbird shapes in varying iridescent colors hanging from a hook in the ceiling and the chimes hanging from it. It looked rather gaudy, but it had a nice tinkling sound when it moved.

"I also got a wonderful pumpkin lantern with a candle. When she went to put that back into the box, she had the base on where the top should be and she put the top onto the base. It was another puzzle to figure out. Now I have a treasure all ready to go out onto the garden table for summer evenings."

Lydia rolled her eyes. "And she wrapped these things up for you?" she asked.

"Ya know," continued her grandmother, "it isn't what the items are, where they came from or how expensive they are. It's the intention in which they were given that counts. Like friends coming for tea and cookies and good conversation, it is they who are the gift no matter how little, insignificant or inconvenient you may think it is. And sometimes these people show up when you most need them, and many times you don't even know it."

Eugenia was remembering fondly the gift Nancy had given Father last year. A broad smile lit her face as she thought of the huge box of *Whitman's Sampler Assorted Chocolates*. The only thing was that Nancy had opened the box and taken every one of the cremes from the assortment, replacing them with a gumdrop. Nancy loved the cremes but not the nut clusters or the caramels, so she left them in the box. She had replaced the lid carefully and wrapped the assortment in red and white foil gift wrap and a velvet bow and had given it to Father for Christmas.

"Nancy grew up in extreme, dire circumstances. Circumstances that I wouldn't wish on my worst enemy. Many times, those behaviors learned when young carry over into adulthood. So, before I judge her or make fun of her, as many do around here, I am reminded just where she came from, and I just smile, consider the source, and send love. She has an enormous heart and good intentions," said Eugenia, sadly.

Lydia looked thoughtful. "I'm beginning to see that," she said. "Are those four new mugs?"

"Yes. Ginger didn't have too, but they sure are pretty. I feel bad though," said Eugenia.

Her granddaughter looked at her with questioning eyes.

"Well," said Eugenia," This is the house where mugs come to die."

January

Chapter Forty-Three

He liked this feeling of contentment; it was different. The men he worked with were easy to get along with and they joked and laughed a lot. Some of the jokes fell on him. He was the first to admit being socially awkward. He was trying to ward off the feeling that sometimes overwhelmed him, the desperation, the urge to hurt, to maim and kill when someone offended him. Yes, he was liking this contentment a lot. He found he could take a lot of teasing as well as give it out.

He now had a shaved head, a full beard and wore glasses, flannel shirts and jeans with heavy, steel toe boots and wool socks. He went by the name of Garry...Garry Phelps. The work was hot, tiring and he was in constant motion. Most nights he didn't dream, he was usually so tired he fell right asleep. Morning bell was at 5:00 am and they were due at the woodlot by seven. Dress, eat and then into the woods. Yes, he was a full-fledged lumberjack now and he liked it.

~

The school session was back in full swing and so was basketball season. Newspaper reporters plagued the school to the point that all visitors were screened before entering the school. Miss Goodwin gave out passes. Any visitor seeing a particular student had only a few minutes and they were not to disturb any student during classes. The more games the boys won the worse it got.

Gale force winds raked the raw and frozen ground. This was Lydia's least favorite month. Cold, icy and dark it afforded no time for outdoor activity unless you were bundled up to the point that it was an extreme effort just to move. The police department's main activities were traffic accidents, a few complaints about domestic violence, missing pets or thefts. The FBI was tracking down leads. More and more missing persons were being discovered that could be a link to Garrett Sellers and his murderous sprees across the south.

Differently Double

Chapter Forty-Four

"Well, who's going to do it? Who will be appointed?" Claire wailed. Dennis, his book in hand, was checking out at the counter of the small village library. "We just can't go on without a historian in this town. It's been a year; what are they dragging their feet for?"

"It gets lonely in there with just me as the librarian and with Ben's death, his office is vacated. I just wanted to keep you on your toes," continued Claire.

"Ask someone at the museum if they want to take on the job," said Dennis, who was the local attorney. "I'll ask at the next town board meeting, but I hear we may have a victim."

Claire was starting to get upset. "You need an attitude adjustment," she said, not taking her eyes off his. "It is a calling, not a job. Get over it."

He scowled. "Well, it doesn't pay all that much, but the town gives you an office."

"But it's important," she interjected. "Just look at the history we have here, especially during the Revolutionary War and the French and Indian Wars, not to mention the genealogy end of it."

"Yeah and it's a lot of hours if someone wants to do it right," he said thoughtfully.

"You of all people know you have to have one, state law and all."

"Yeah, yeah," he remarked.

She looked critically at him and he met her gaze. "Things are getting you down," she said.

"Ok, ok reading me again huh. I'm knee-deep in the Dottie thing. With defense strategy and partnering up with that law firm I found in Mobile, I've got a lot on my mind. When her case breaks, it will be national news, and here we go again. Shades of years past."

"Dennis, I'm always reading you. You're a big barrel of fun to read."

"I wish I could put a stopper on that gift of yours, but no laws out there to do it with," he said, smiling slyly at her.

"Dennis, you're my cousin and I'm concerned. Besides, we can joke about it."

He hugged her, sighed and left the library by the side door, but not before telling Claire that he liked her Christmas decorations.

Claire looked back to see Olivia and Lydia standing at the small card catalog. They were both smiling and looking at Dennis's retreating back as he made his way toward the barbershop.

"Time to get roasted and toasted," Claire muttered. Something the regulars in the barbershop were good at.

Olivia and Lydia just giggled and approached the counter to check out their books.

Chapter Forty-Five

"Have a place for me to stay," Nancy anxiously said as she pushed her way into Eugenia's kitchen. She looked nervous and upset. It was bitter cold and although sunny, the snow and ice stayed on the ground making going very treacherous. Sidewalks were sanded and people wore good shoes with traction, some even had cleats attached to their shoes. The local snowshoe club had weekly outings on Saturdays to places where one would usually hike in nicer weather, but the down and out hikers usually didn't let the weather get in the way. Many would tell you the best time to hike or snowshoe was in a snowstorm. The quietness of the woods and the gently falling snow gave one a sense of peace and tranquility. The abandoned roads in the State Lands were a treasure for snowshoeing.

"Now what the hell happened?" said Eugenia, "I didn't see you drive up."

"No, I walked."

"You walked?" said Lydia and Olivia in unison. They were sitting at the kitchen table, sorting out some coupons for Eugenia.

"Mind the dates," Eugenia said to the girls referring to the expiration dates of the coupons before she turned her attention back to Nancy.

Nancy looked like she was going to burst into tears at any moment. She removed her gloves and hat and opened her heavy coat. Her boots made small puddles on the kitchen floor.

"Why did you walk, you usually drive?" said Eugenia.

"I know, but when my husband gets home, he's going to divorce me."

"Sit down and I'll brew some tea."

Nancy sat down heavily with a deep sigh. Lydia and Olivia, both sitting at the table, put their chins in their hands and stared at her. She looked back at them, a resigned and disgusted look on her face. "What are you looking at?" she said defensively.

Eugenia plopped two sugars in the cup and a teabag, covered the bag with boiling water and set the cup in front of Nancy. "It's black tea, good for your soul," remarked Eugenia.

"Right now I feel like I don't have a body or a mind, let alone a soul," she said. "Well, I wasn't paying attention" both girls looked at one another and raised their eyebrows. "And I didn't realize the garage door was down. I backed right through it."

"Uhoooo," said Olivia.

"Ouch," said Lydia

"Shit happens," said Eugenia trying to keep a straight face and from bursting out laughing.

"No, it doesn't," wailed Nancy. "He'll kill me. I'm so disgusted with myself. Last week I fell asleep at the bridge and hit the guard rail. Now, this!"

"Ok, I think you have a problem. I know you have a problem," said Eugenia. "So, how's your sleep?"

"Not good," said Nancy, "I seem to get all my sleep in the afternoon. I doze or catnap. I can't get to sleep at night, no matter how hard I try. I'm always up at 2:00 am."

"Have you seen the doctor about it?"

"Yes, they say it's hormones, so they give me pills. I go back two months later, things haven't changed. They give me more pills and on it goes. I'm just so frustrated."

"Have they got you into the sleep lab yet?" asked Eugenia.

"What's that? Oh, the sleep apnea thing, the mask and all that. No," Nancy sipped her tea and looked dejectedly at the table.

"I think it's about time. If you can't get it done at the main hospital here go to one of the satellite ones," said Eugenia. "The sooner the better."

"What mask?" asked Olivia.

"It's hooked to a machine that helps you breathe during the night," explained Eugenia.

Eugenia casually sipped her tea and setting the cup carefully down said, "Some people can't sleep because of medical problems like sleep apnea. It has several underlying causes and some are physical, but the main problem is the upper airway into the lungs narrows while sleeping. This causes snoring, but most importantly blocked airways cause you to wake many times during the night. You can't get a good night's rest.

There are tests for that now. People have been able to get a good night's sleep who haven't had one in years by using a CPAP machine."

Both girls looked interested, especially knowing one more little thing about Nancy. This put her into a whole new perspective.

Differently Double

February

Chapter Forty-Six

The end of February signaled the semi-annual cleaning of the manure storage at Howard's farm. Huge tractors hauling large-wheeled vehicles that held the slurry from the manure pits could be encountered at all hours of the day in the streets through town. The large manure spreaders were headed toward fields that would be planted when the weather was better. Now, most of the fields were still frozen and even though many were devoid of snow the tractors were not likely to become stuck in the mud. The wind blew relentlessly and cold still permeated the nights. Warmth in the just-above-freezing temperatures during the day and the anticipation of daylight savings time afforded some hope for the locals.

Howard, driving one of the huge tractors that could crush a normal car with one wheel, was going a little too fast past the bank and as usual, he was talking on his cell phone. Unbeknown to him, a State Trooper followed. Just as Howard passed the town garage and approached the village limits sign, the State Trooper put on his lights in an attempt to pull him over.

Howard, momentarily taken by surprise, became a little disoriented and instead of disengaging his forward speed he accidentally hit the lever to engage the system to unload the spreader. Just as Howard came to a complete stop, the spreader had managed to unload more than a ton of liquid, rich manure all over the road, completely engulfing the trooper car.

Needless to say, Howard was in a lot of trouble.

Chris received the call first. *Trooper stuck in his car, unable to exit.*

"Can't he just drive out of it," whined Chris, a smirk on his face. "Christ, go to the damned car wash and come back. Howard's not going anywhere." Matt edged further toward his boss. He couldn't believe what he was hearing. A trooper stuck in his car?

"Yeah," said Chris, "a State Boy's car just got buried in manure, compliments of Howard." Chris tried to have composure, but he was laughing so hard that he had to turn and walk into his office and slam the door.

"Ya don't piss Howard off," said one of the secretaries, who was enlisting all her friends to go with her during lunch break to see the mess.

Meanwhile, calls were coming in from the scene and dispatch was on the radio to several patrol cars. Traffic control was needed and Chris might have to call the Environmental Conservation Department if the county deemed it a pollution hazard.

Chapter Forty-Seven

Eugenia's battered old sedan tore up Nancy's driveway, which was currently paved with ice. Eugenia drove her car at two speeds: fast and slow. There was no in-between. Nancy and her husband lived outside of town near Howard's farm. Eugenia usually picked Nancy up for their twice-weekly sojourns to the senior meal site where they helped prepare the meals for the local senior citizens. This time, Lydia and Olivia were in the back seat as it was school conference day and they had been convinced to help out.

"What's wrong with your glasses?" Eugenia asked Nancy, as she got into the car.

Nancy removed her glasses and looked at them. "Oh God, they're bad aren't they?" She sighed. "Oh well, I cleaned them before I brushed my teeth."

"Yeah, so what?" retorted Eugenia.

"Well, I did my *on the run* cleaning on them," she answered.

"Your what?" said Eugenia, now thoroughly confused.

"You know *if you're in doubt and find yourself without...lick em!*" said Nancy, matter-of-factly.

"Oh for God's sake," screeched Eugenia, "no wonder you can't see."

Olivia and Lydia both chorused "eek."

"Tell me you didn't have peanut butter for breakfast," asked Lydia, hopefully.

"How did you know?" inquired an astonished Nancy.

"Oh my God," screeched Lydia putting her head in her hands.

Olivia reached into her pocket and produced a Zeiss Lens Cleaning towelette. "I don't go without these, now that I'm learning photography," she said haughtily. "Here, use this."

Nancy reached over her head without turning toward the girls and took the wipe. The two girls just rolled their eyes and shook their heads.

"Vacation today?" asked Nancy, casually.

"Yes," said Lydia and looked back at the muddy fields as they passed by.

Differently Double

March

Chapter *Forty-Eight*

Eugenia was standing in Dottie's kitchen yelling at Howard.

"What do you mean you threw him out, he's a Monk for Christ's sake. A holy man."

"Holy my ass," retorted Howard. "Have you seen my rental house?" He was referring to one of his rental properties, the one on the main road just out of town. Whenever Howard purchased a farm and a house came with the property, he would rent it out to anyone in need of a home to live in.

"Yes, I have seen the *Come and get Jesus, Jesus Lives Here, Jesus Saves* and *Safe House* in three-foot letters all over that dump you rent out at the bottom of the hill" shouted Eugenia. "It's right along the highway so you can't miss it. It makes quite a statement. So what?"

Dottie just stood there not believing what she was hearing.

Howard's face was chiseled into a glare and his fists were clenched.

"Well, you should see the inside walls. If you like subway graffiti, man that's the place," he shouted. "Now I have to get someone, somehow to paint the place inside and out. I came here for encouragement and you accost me as soon as I enter the damn door."

"Ok, ok, let's have a cool down," said Dottie quietly. "Both of you."

Howard sighed and said, "Listen, in my defense I did everything possible for him. I called the monastery, the one he's supposed to be affiliated with. They said they threw him out of there several years ago and that if he goes off his medicine, watch out. He owes me three months' back rent and a paint job and whatever else."

Staring at Eugenia, Dottie said, "Here is my point. I know what he did at the tavern night before last. I mean the whole town is talking about it. I mean a monk is not supposed to go after women at a bar. Period. The thought of it provokes me."

"And pinching her in the ass," injected Howard, smugly.

Dottie continued, "what if he was alone with one of our children, what then? I mean helping himself to a patron at the local bar as she walks past is one thing, but what if it was one of our children? Can you imagine?"

"And," Howard injected, "when the boyfriend found out and got hold of him, hell, the whole bar got hold of him and they did a job on him, but..."

"Point taken," sighed Eugenia, her voice elevated to a shriek.

"Now I feel vindicated," said Howard, smugly. "Any more cookies and milk? Well, any more cookies?"

"I just wanted to hear about the latest escapade of that monk, that's all," said Eugenia, as she threw her hands in the air and marched past Howard onto the back porch, slamming the door behind her.

"Wipe the smirk off your face, Howard," said Dottie quietly, but Howard was already laughing heartily.

Chapter Forty-Nine

His small campfire was smoky, to say the least. He had a few more days of food in his army- issued knapsack, but that was all. Enough to get him by. He was feeling very down, almost suicidal again. He wasn't supposed to feel this way...why him? He did have a split lip and a bruise on one cheekbone, but no broken bones this time.

"Every time I pray to you, you get me into trouble," muttered the monk as he fingered his crucifix. His brown woolen robe fitted his slight frame modestly and although it was filthy, it covered him on this cold, windy, spring day. "I'm filled with the devil," he sighed, "and no one to help. Hell, I can't even help myself."

He felt the presence first and then he saw them; two boys and a man. They just stood there watching him.

"We saw the smoke, and thought it was a fire," said the tall, stout boy.

"I live just over the hill from here, how about a bed in my antique shop for the night?" Gene told him. "Just no graffiti."

The monk looked wearily at them and nodded. "Word travels fast," he muttered.

"Well your arts-man-ship couldn't go unnoticed," said Gene, flippantly. He smiled at the lone man, pitying him.

The monk climbed wearily up from his seat on the grass, stubbed out his small fire, grabbed his pack and followed them.

"Oh, I'm Gene and this is Kenny and Louis."

The monk nodded and extended a hand.

"I have a feeling you will have supper brought out before you're there twenty minutes," said Gene. "My landlady will get every ounce of history out of you within ten minutes and you won't know what hit you."

"History, I don't have one," sighed the monk. "I wish I did, but I'm one of those abandoned ones; even Jesus doesn't like me."

"I find that hard to believe," said Gene, quietly.

"Jesus is about love and forgiveness," said Kenny.

"And gratitude," Louis chimed in.

[171]

"Yes, but when he abandons you, you have nothing."

"Yes, you do," injected Kenny. "He never abandons you. Besides you always have yourself and that's the best part."

"Myself is a delectable mix of contradictions," the monk stated.

"No one has to live this way. Why don't you go see Father Munro, he's a spirit man. A Catholic priest," said Gene. "There's also his friend Dr. Menzies who helps him. Menzies is only a phone call away and Father lives right in the village. Those two could help you."

"Yes," both boys said in unison.

And so it was that the monk came to stay at Gene's antique shop for a total of two weeks. He kept busy dusting and labeling antiques, all the while talking of places he had been and people who he knew. On the day he was to leave he headed to town to see Father Munro and then onto parts unknown. Mrs. Henderson packed snacks, sandwiches, and cookies. Gene and several of the ladies in town made sure he had extra warm clothing and a jacket and that his robe was washed and packed in his backpack.

The late morning sunlight filtered through the blinds in the small sitting room, illuminating the tiny blue pattern on the teacups that sat on the small table near two men huddled in deep conversation

"First of all, what is your name? I know you're a monk, but you're Brother...?" said Father looking expectantly at the man sitting next to him.

"Brother John," came the quiet reply from the man with the sad eyes who sat across from him.

"The torture und abuse has been with you for so long you've forgotten how to live a life free of them. If you have a good day you feel guilty und if you have a bad day, it's all part of the course. Am I not right?" said Father tentatively.

The monk nodded, frowning.

"And so, we have Jesus as our savior, but how can Jesus or, for that matter, God or even yourself save you if you don't take that first step for change. God's love is all about change. He'll show you the way, but you must take that first step. I see a man who all he does is feel sorry for himself und the world, instead of looking at all the good there is in it und all the things he can do to change things for the better. But moderation is the byword here, not full, in-your-face evangelism. That just doesn't work. People get turned off by it. The message is gotten across by deeds, not words."

"I'm a monk, for God's sake," said Brother John.

"Und at the moment you shouldn't be one. You are too passionate und you have a lot of baggage that's not being addressed. It's just shoved aside. This isn't your calling at the moment, for God has healing in mind for you. You can't heal others until you heal yourself. When you start loving yourself, then the love flows to all others."

"Stop running," were the last words Father said to him as he turned to go.

As Brother John stepped from the porch, dead leaves crackled under his feet as he shuffled from the sidewalk to the road and headed west toward somewhere.

Father looked for a long time at the lone figure of the man, already fading from sight.

~

"Son of a bitch," muttered Howard as he saw the thin figure ambling down the road in front of him. He was on a lonely stretch of county road several miles from his farm and he had a full load of manure. His tractor roared under the load of the heavy liquid enclosed in its temporary home.

His first inclination was to pull the lever and send a wash of manure all over the lone figure, but then he felt bad for wishing that on anyone.

The monk looked up and gave him a furtive glance as he passed. Howard gave the man plenty of space on the road and in about twenty yards he stopped his vehicle and climbed down the steep steps of the tractor. He held a large paper sack in his hand and he extended it to the man who now was walking slowly, hesitantly toward him.

"Here are some cookies and a few sandwiches. I'm sorry things didn't work out," said Howard.

"I can't possibly take this, it's your lunch, "said Brother John.

"Yes, you can," said Howard. "All I have to do is go back and beg some more, or better yet just look like my hungry indomitable self and food just appears." Howard looked thoughtfully at the man who stood in front of him and said: "You remind me of me in my younger days."

Brother John laughed. "That would be a surprise," he said, slowly.

"Na, I just couldn't get away from myself so I learned to live with me. You have to do the same. Ya know, ya just have to face your demons. Don't run from them and don't try to hide, that's just futile shit."

"Good advice," said Brother John, with a sad smile. "I'm still running, but someday I'll slow down."

"I'm in the slowdown mode but still running myself," Howard said sadly.

~

It was late afternoon and the sun cast long shadows along the road. The fields were greening and soon corn and soybean planting would be underway. The air was getting warmer and the days were getting longer in this part of New York State.

Brother John heard the rumbling noise in the distance but paid no attention until the truck drew up alongside him. The truck was full of logs and the tangy smell of fresh-cut pulp wood assailed his nostrils. It was the pleasant smell of balsa and pine mixed with damp earth.

The fully bearded, tall and lanky driver yelled out the passenger side window. "Want a ride? I'm going to the mill bout an hour away."

Brother John opened the door, climbed the steps up into the cab and looked into the two most malevolent eyes he could ever imagine.

Differently Double

Differently Double

Chapter Fifty

Mandy entered the café with her mother. Everyone knew Mandy at the café. When her mother brought her in, about once a week, Suzie Evans, one of the owners, would dote on her and give her a free ice cream soda, her favorite. But today, Mandy was truly agitated.

Her mother, Ginger looked cautiously at Suzie, "funny"' she said, "she was all happy to come here and then when she got to the door, something happened and she wanted to go home. Said something about a dark man in here and she was afraid. She kept saying dark man, dark man."

"Hum," said Suzie, "place is busy, a few tourists, some regulars and of course Nathan's crew. They're a bunch of jokers those guys. Real charmers," she said sarcastically.

Mandy now openly clawed at her mother and wanted her to pick her up.

"I'll take a rain check," said Ginger. She turned and hurried for the door. Mandy was now openly staring at the group of men who were working for Nathan. Her mother had to drag her out the door of the café.

They all saw the little girl's reaction and this elicited another round of jokes from the crew like, "Hey, who didn't take a shower this morning," or "I knew we were an ugly bunch but this is ridiculous."

Suzie just looked at all of them, shook her head and headed for the coffee pot.

Differently Double

Chapter Fifty-One

The urges were coming on strong again. The voices, why couldn't he fight them? He had basked momentarily in serenity, peace, and the jovial company of others. That's all he wanted was peace. Peace from the demons that haunted him and peace in his world, but he had a job to finish and finish it he must.

~

"Hey Mom," yelled Lydia, "we're home."

"So soon," exclaimed Karen.

"Well, we had a problem," she said.

"Let's sit down with cookies and milk and we'll discuss it," said Karen.

The three kids sat in chairs and devoured half the tin of homemade chocolate chip cookies telling their story between mouthfuls.

"We were in the woods today," said Olivia "and we were walking toward the old stone circle. You know, just at the part where the path splits. The timber guys are in the other section now, cutting trees."

Karen nodded.

Lydia continued the story. "Well, we were talking and joking and we were a little loud and all of a sudden this little girl comes up to us. She's the same one I've been seeing lately. You know, the ghost. Anyway, she comes up to us and we were scared. We could kinda see right through her."

"Oh, for God's sake, she's a ghost and we saw her," exclaimed Olivia with a disgusted look on her face.

Karen carefully put her cup down and nodded for them to continue.

"Well, Kenny says to her, what do you want?"

"Well, she wants us to follow her and she leads us into this brushy place. I mean it's dense and scratchy. She says to us, I mean in our heads, *"hide here and make no sound until he goes."*

"That's true," said Kenny and Olivia, simultaneously.

Lydia continued, "We are all standing there looking at one another when O hears something like a twig snap. Well, we all crouch down and, in a few minutes, this guy comes along. He has a rope in one hand and a rock in the other. He picks up one rock and throws it down and picks up another almost as if he's collecting certain rocks. I've seen him in town, but I don't know where. It looked like he was following us, just the way he was walking, listening..."

"Like he was tracking us," remarked Kenny.

"Well, when he passed us, the girl follows him. Scared us real bad. We waited for a few minutes and then we all got out of there and ran here," said Olivia.

Karen felt cold fingers of fear on her neck and sweat beaded on her forehead. She called Matt and told him the news.

Chapter Fifty-Two

Gene's sleep was troubled. He woke up several times covered in sweat. The dreams and the feeling of imminent doom in the pit of his stomach happened every few days now and they were accelerating.

The last time he woke from his fitful sleep he knew that something had happened, but what and to whom? In the dream, he saw a large truck and the figure of a man climbing up and up unending steps trying to get into the cab of the truck. Blood was everywhere. Then the dream switched to a dark forest, brooding and menacing.

Now, fully awake his eyes settled on a spot at the foot of the bed and there stood the luminous figure of a small child. She was wearing a sundress and she was smiling at him. He squeezed his eyes closed and when he opened them, she was gone.

He rolled over and sat up, momentarily dazed. His hand grazed his thin stubble of beard as he reached up to rub the sleep from his eyes. God, he felt like he hadn't slept in months. His heart raced, his mouth was dry and he had to pee.

"Shit," he said to himself, "might as well get up."

As he pulled the cover away from his sweating body his mind brought him back to the previous day at the shop. He remembered he was looking for something in the back room. The front doorbells rang with their resounding clanks and tinkles, alerting him that someone had just come into the shop. When he looked, there was no one there. The door was closed, but one of the bells was still swinging from the leather tie that suspended it just above the door. He remembered attributing it to the wind, but as he chanced to look in the direction of the old wood stove where a beam of sunlight had momentarily shone on the old, polished wood floor, there stood the figure of a small child. She vanished as quickly as she appeared. He was momentarily shaken, then he remembered Katie's words, "You'll have help, it just may not be what you expect."

"It's bad enough with the nightmares, now ghosts? What next?" he muttered to himself as he made his way to the bathroom in the predawn light.

~

Father came to see Gene early that morning. Father knew, deep down, that the end was near. The showdown was beginning. Menzies, who had returned to the area, was also concerned.

"We could hospitalize you," Menzies told Gene.

"No," said Gene, "I have to face this one. I have to face him."

April

Chapter Fifty-Three

It was early the next morning and Ginger had banking business to do. Mandy walked beside her mother who had promised to take her fishing after the bank errand. In front of the bank, Ginger noticed a large truck parked with its motor running. The truck was filled with logs. When Ginger saw the truck, her grip tightened on Mandy's hand. Mandy stopped and began to squirm violently as a tall, thin man exited the bank.

Mandy shouted, "there he is, the Dark Man, the Dark Man."

The man nodded his head to Ginger and looked angrily at Mandy, as he got into the passenger side of the truck and it drove away.

This was the second time that Mandy had encountered someone she called the *Dark Man*. Ginger was concerned so after the bank visit, they visited Matt at the police station on their way to the fishing site. Ginger told Matt of the encounter while Dave listened. This was the second time that this had happened and they both knew Mandy.

"Why would she say that?" they asked.

They began to question her, first asking who was the Dark Man.

At first, Mandy just looked confused, then she said "oh, oh, he is a mean, evil man. He is here to hurt us."

Later that morning, Ginger took Mandy fishing, but Mandy's interests seemed to be elsewhere.

"Pearly Pond, Pearly Pond," sang Mandy as she threw stones into the glimmering water of the Fish and Game Club pond.

"Momma," she said, "I want to go and visit Terd."

"You mean Ferd, your friend Dottie's horse?" questioned Ginger.

Mandy shook her head yes. "He's our friend Momma. He's going to save us."

Cold fingers of sweat crept down Ginger's back when she heard this comment.

Mandy was now softly singing a little ditty that unnerved Ginger to the core, "Terd will save us, Terd, Terd, save us Terd."

Chapter Fifty-Four

Gene entered the cafe and sat at the counter. It was quiet now, but the lunchtime crowd would be coming momentarily. He felt eyes drill into him, prying, curious eyes, and he glanced around and saw four men sitting at a booth in the corner near the front window. They were having lunch. He looked at each one. They were all clean-shaven but one. His eyes bored into the only man with a beard. Recognition, but where? The stranger was as shocked as he was to see him, he could tell. That face, those eyes, he knew he was one of the local timber crew. Somehow this guy stood out from the rest like he didn't belong with them. They teased him and he seemed to get his comments in when the conversation heated up, but there was something... Gene listened. That voice! He recognized that voice, soft but deep, menacing, just like his father's voice.

He turned away, his face burning. He felt ill, but he had to keep all vestiges of it to himself. He had to look as nonchalantly as possible, as he didn't want the man to know he recognized him. This wasn't the long lost brother you could just hang around and be friends with.

He thought, wasn't he the one Mandy was so upset by? When Ginger came to see him yesterday about fixing the wheel on a toy wagon, she mentioned the men from the logging company and Mandy's reaction to one of them. The one with the beard.

Suzie came up to the counter. He smiled at her.

"Little under the weather, Gene?" she asked.

"Naw, just tired," he said. "Tomato soup and grilled cheese, please. Oh, and a hot chocolate."

"Comin' right up," said Suzie.

Placing his hand on Gene's shoulder, Roger Eckerson sidled up to him at the counter.

"My lamp done?" he inquired.

"Yes," said Gene. "I'll be back in the shop at one."

"See you then," said Roger, taking a seat behind him at a booth where two women waited.

He heard the men getting up from their seats and heading for the front door. The man with the beard lagged a little behind. Gene made a point not to look at him, for this might just give him away, or cement the man's recognition of him. Momentarily, he glanced at the back of the man in the lead then turned his head back to look straight in front of him. His face was flushed and he was glad there weren't mirrors on the back wall of the cafe. This could have given the bearded man a chance to see how uncomfortable he was. He felt the man's eyes momentarily bore into his back and then they were all out on the sidewalk, walking toward their trucks.

He let out a deep sigh. Now, what to do. He knew he wasn't safe. Just then he heard the tinkling of the bell at the front door. Matt walked in with his partner Joe.

Gene looked at him and said, "you're just the one I wanna see."

He told them about the encounter and how sure he was about the identity of Garrett.

"Let's keep this quiet to the locals," said Matt in a hushed voice. "I know the FBI guys are gonna want to tail him without him knowing. I'll tell Dave when I get back to the station. No sense calling it in from here. Hell, the whole town'll know before I get the second sentence out."

"He's diabolical," said Gene. "He'll know."

"We just don't want any more incidents; that's the bottom line," said Joe.

~

Matt looked at Gene quizzically. "You all right?" he asked.

Gene was looking for words in which to tell Matt and Joe his experiences of the past few days. He hesitated, "well, it's the dreams and the feelings now, plus," he hesitated and continued, "that wouldn't be bad enough, but now I have a ghost."

"Oh no, not again," sighed Joe, putting his coffee cup down and wiping his forehead with his hand.

Matt let out a deep breath, "let me guess," he said, "a little girl in a sundress."

Gene looked at Matt in shock. "Yessss," he said, cautiously.

"My sister," said Matt, sadly. "Her name is Selma. She's here to help. Garrett killed her many years ago. I miss her so much." Tears welled in Matt's eyes as he rubbed his hand through his curly hair. Both men just looked at him in shock. "Long story," he continued, "but Garrett has been on my radar for a long, long time. I want this bastard."

Differently Double

Chapter Fifty-Five

He had discovered a man in town who looked just like him. His encounter gave him a high he never knew he could achieve. It was his long lost brother; his twin. His death would be the ultimate accomplishment of his life. He was now planning the end; their final elimination...all of them.

~

"Hey Dan," said Suzie. "Coffee?"

"Yup," came the reply from a short, stocky man in his mid-sixties.

"Goin' hunting?" she inquired.

"I'm takin' the wheeler out now. My grandson will follow when he comes home from school."

He nodded to Howard and said, "I'm going up unto the south slope to check for those coyotes and anything more I can find up there."

Howard nodded and replied, "yeah, they're sure bothering Charlie's sheep. Heard he lost three last night and two the night before."

"Why doesn't he just get one of those dogs that live with the sheep. They're expensive, but maybe it could help," replied a customer.

"I hear they're using donkeys," said another of the patrons sitting at the counter.

"Next it will be ostriches," shouted another, laughing.

"Give it up guys," shouted Suzie over the din. "More coffee?"

Differently Double

Chapter Fifty-Six

Dan gunned the motor, but when the wheeler slid backward down the small side hill he was negotiating, he decided to park and go on foot. He noticed vultures circling. Some were on the ground, hopping to and fro, about one hundred feet from where he stood. They were picking at what was left, he supposed of some poor carcass. Their incessant hissing made him shiver.

"Blasted things," he muttered.

He turned and started up the trail away from the feeding frenzy. The snowpack was light in the dense woods and had already disappeared from the fields. He made his way up the slope to one of his blinds in a deep stand of oaks. He listened and looked skyward. Several vultures still circled the area.

"Hum," he thought, "I wonder if something got one of Charlie's sheep, dragged it up here and partially ate it?"

After looking around, he made his way back down the slope. The air was crisp and assailed his nostrils with the clean scent of pine and balsa. He stopped occasionally and inhaled the damp earthy smell of dead leaves and loamy soil. He loved the woods. He loved being here and feeling the coming of spring.

He heard the sound of the wheeler before he saw it. His grandson was coming up the trail so he hurried toward the sound. Parking beside the wheeler, his grandson Jamie dismounted and joined his grandfather who was coming down the slope toward him.

"Hey, I want you to come here and we'll get those vultures the hell outta here and see what they're scrapping over," Dan yelled to his ten-year-old grandson. "Hear 'em hissing at one another?"

The boy laughed and said, "yeah, we learned in class that turkey vultures don't have voice boxes so all they can do is hiss. It's an eerie sound. Got your gun?"

"Yeah, in case I needed it up on the hill."

He continued, "Those vultures could be nasty if we try to get a look at their prey. Let's just see if it's one of Charlie's sheep left by the coyotes."

Vultures, eight of them hopped on the ground, hissing at one another and displaying their six-foot wingspans when Dan and his grandson approached.

"What the Hell?" said Dan. "I don't like this."

"Ohhh crap," whined his grandson, who was looking at something on the ground about ten feet away from the commotion made by the birds and almost at his feet.

"Shit, is it...is it?" Jamie clutched his stomach and turned as if to vomit. His mouth was dry and he couldn't catch his breath, as he backed a few steps away.

Dan just stared at the open eye sockets and the tufts of unruly hair on the head of the human skull at his grandson's feet.

He turned toward his grandson and gasped, "Go git help. Hurry," he said gruffly.

"I'm gonna back against this tree and probably puke," Dan muttered.

"Be careful, ya got your cell?" Jamie called as he ran toward the wheeler.

"Yeah, but it doesn't work here on this side of the mountain. Just git the hell goin, I don't like this," he shouted as he chambered a round in his twelve gauge.

He heard the wheeler start and then descend the hill toward the road. He heard its distant roar fading and the quiet of the woods engulfed him once again. It was getting toward dusk and the vultures were leaving for their roost in an old tree just over the body. The cold was descending. "Who in the hell is it?" he asked himself as he stayed rooted to the base of a large white pine tree, the coarse feel of its bark a welcome feel on his back.

Just then a howl split the air with surreal intensity. A howl he knew too well. The pack was descending on his little party in the woods. Then he heard it; small hesitant footsteps accompanied by growls and short yips. He had to protect this body. He peeked around the base of the tree. There were three of them, but the rest of the pack he was sure wasn't far behind. He shouldered his gun and took a bead on the lead coyote. He was all of sixty pounds, he judged. Large for a coyote. With his trained eye, he noticed this one, in particular, had a much broader face and was much darker in the body than most. He pushed the safety lever to off and gently squeezed the trigger. The retort from the gun was deafening and the vultures rose into the air. The sound from the gun rolled down the valley in graduating undulations. The pack scattered, all except the lead one; the dead one. "They'll be back, but not today," he thought.

Differently Double

Chapter Fifty-Seven

Dan's grandson burst into the police station. He was dirty and wet. "Help," he screamed, "dead body in the woods."

Chris bolted from his desk.

"Where, Jamie?" he said.

"Up with Grandpa. He's protecting it. It's getting dark," he gasped

"All available," Chris shouted to dispatch. "Want to show us where?" he said, turning toward the boy.

"Yeah, but you're not gonna get cars up there," said Jamie.

"Get the fire department and the ambulance, they have wheelers. Call them out now," shouted Chris. He grabbed his heavyweight parka from the hook. "I'll follow you," he told the boy.

"Where," screamed the dispatcher, as policemen filed past him and out into the twilight.

"In the woods just beyond the old Miller place. First fencerow. You'll see the wheeler tracks. It's an abandoned road that ends up in the woods before it gets steep," said Jamie.

The dispatcher nodded his head, knowing exactly where the scene was.

Chris put a hand on Jamie's shoulder.

"You ok?" he asked, concern in his voice.

The boy nodded and headed out the door.

As they stepped outside, they heard the distant retort of a shotgun. "That's got to be Gramps," said Jamie. "Oh God, I hope he's all right." He was shaking violently.

"Let's go," said Chris.

"K1 to base, we're on it," said Matt who, along with his partner Joe, were speeding toward the scene from the opposite direction.

Approaching the road, Joe mumbled, "oh man look at the mud. I'm not dressed for this."

"Wish I had my knee boots," mumbled Matt.

They heard the distant whine of motors and suddenly the road was full of four-wheelers, along with the local ambulance and Larry's four-wheel-drive Jeep he always went to work with. Larry stopped beside the squad car with the two men in it and yelled, "get in. I can make it most of the way with this."

Chris immediately pulled alongside, stopped his car and also jumped into the Jeep, barely getting the door closed before Larry took off. Chris said excitedly, "Let the kid lead with the wheeler; he's been there."

Then turning to Larry, Chris said, "You're quick."

"Intercepted the call on Steve's scanner and when I heard body, well...I bolted for the door."

"Got your gun safety on?" asked Chris. He was smiling, remembering several years previous when four policemen were crammed into a small all-terrain vehicle going to a crime scene and one of the rookie officers forgot to secure his gun. With the rough terrain, the gun became partially dislodged from its holster and discharged, shooting the rookie's toe off. Chris still remembered that. It was still a very big point of contention with him. Only service revolvers on the job. No exceptions, don't care if the gun was in the Battle of the Bighorn. Only service revolvers. Period!

Matt was sitting next to the guy at the time and remembered the incident fondly. "Marvin, the folly of the Emeryville Police Department," he said laughing.

"More like Barney Fife," retorted Larry. "I had to work lab with the guy. When he passed out while I was showing him a corpse, I knew he wouldn't last long."

"That was a long night in the hospital," remarked Joe, shaking his head. "I had to go hold his hand."

"Yeah, and I still remember the mountain of paperwork after," muttered Chris.

~

The small four-wheeler with Jamie in control carefully negotiated the ruts and potholes in the muddy road and parked by a larger four-wheeler at the base of a small hill leading up into a heavily wooded slope.

"We walk from here," said the boy as he approached the Jeep.

Dark was fast approaching and flashlights gleamed through the impending darkness.

"Gramps," called the boy.

"Still here," came a hoarse reply.

"I heard a gun."

"Shot a coyote," came the answer.

The group arrived and Aron, the local EMT, and Larry approached the body.

"Head's over there," said Jamie, pointing to a dark object several feet from the body.

"Oh shit," came a terse retort from one of the local squad.

"Recognize him?" asked Joe.

"Yeah, I think it's that monk guy. At least I think I recognize my coat."

"Your coat?" said Matt, incredulously.

"Your wife had a small clothing drive for the monk before he left town. I gave her my coat. I wasn't wearing it because I got a new one for Christmas and you can only wear one coat at a time," he said defensively.

"I figured," he continued, "as long as he was leaving the area might as well let bygones be bygones. I was the one who threw the first punch that night at the tavern. I admit it. Got thrown out of there because of it. That son-of-a-bitch Artie still wouldn't let me back in until the other day and then he gives me a free beer. Go figure," he muttered, shaking his head from side to side.

"All right, secure the spot. We need floods up here," said Chris.

"I'll snake up the lines for the spots," said Aron, "he's been dead awhile, you won't need us."

"Not so fast," said Larry. "I can see from here he's been dragged. Those damned vultures are strong, but to remove a head takes some doing. I'm getting more than just vultures here. Coyotes, bobcats, wolves something large enough to chew through the backbone. Too early for bear yet. We got this body just in time."

Dan sidled up to Larry, "come take a look at this coyote I just shot. I think you'll be impressed."

Larry followed Dan and so did Matt and Joe. The animal lay on its side, blood congealing on the fur at its chest.

"Christ, that's a big one," said Larry.

"Look at the muzzle and the ears. That's a coy-wolf," Dan said, meaning a wolf/coyote hybrid. "I'll bet my life on it. Ya want the head?"

"Yes," said Larry, hesitating, "just give me the head. I'll compare teeth marks. You keep the rest."

"I'll skin 'em and call ya when I'm done here," said Dan. He called for his grandson, who held the flashlight. Nedo, who had just arrived at the scene was standing nearby. He watched in wonderment as expert hands separated the fur from the rest of the body.

~

Crime scene techs worked diligently under the spotlights which illuminated the ground around the body. They followed a trail to a small spot where the body had been initially dumped. From there, animals had dragged the body, after taking care of much of its meaty and fleshy areas.

The steady hum of generators could be heard as evidence bags were assembled to hold the bits and pieces of clothing, hair, fiber, leaves, soil, and bone. They were collected into one spot and transferred to one of three large tubs so they could be transported to the lab. The skull went into another bag.

All through the night, ladies from the local firemen's auxiliary supplied the workers with hot coffee and cocoa, sandwiches and warm hats, mittens, and jackets.

Larry motioned to Chris, "I'm done here for now," he said wearily. "Take these to the van, I'll work on them in the morning." As Larry looked up he said wearily, "Oh hell, it's today isn't it?"

Tired faces looked up as the first rays of light illuminated the horizon.

Chapter Fifty-Eight

Matt stopped the car in the barnyard of the huge milking complex that was Howards' farm. He got out of the car and proceeded toward the milking parlor as Howard exited the door.

"Well," said Howard, "fancy meeting you here."

"I gotta talk to you," said Matt. "I know you heard about Brother John and I need to ask you some questions."

Howard started to protest, but Matt cut him off.

"Listen, we're conducting this investigation and whether you like it or not, you knew him. You were his landlord. Now, let's get this over with and you can go on about your business. So, when is the last time you saw Brother John?" asked Matt.

Howard looked pensive, his face showed concern. "Well, I was spreading manure and I passed him. He was walking, headed outta town. I stopped and offered him my lunch. Said I was sorry and all and then I went on."

"See anything or anyone else? Anyone follow you?" Matt asked.

Howard blew out a short breath, "not that I recall. If I remember something," he said and then hesitated, frowning. "I can't put my hand on it at the moment, but there was someone behind me...something. Shit, this will bother me all day," he said.

~

That afternoon as Howard exited the bank and stood at the corner waiting to cross the street, he heard the roar of a large engine. As he watched the approaching log truck loaded with logs he thought, "Hell, better not move or I'll be..."

"Shit, that's it," shouted Howard. "A log truck. That's what was following me that day and he slowed down for that monk too."

Howard crossed the street but instead of going to the cafe where he was initially headed, he went to the police station. He entered the door and bellowed for Matt. Chris was at his desk but moved to the front of the reception area with haste.

"What Howard?" he asked.

"Matt asked me a question today. Involves that Monk. Yes, I saw something and it was a log truck, one of the big ones. Probably headed for the mill. It passed me as I pulled into the field out by the old Miller place. Please tell him that."

"Thanks, Howard, this is very good information," remarked Chris.

"Been racking my brains thinking about it. Glad I can be of some help," said Howard as he made his way toward the door.

Chapter Fifty-Nine

"Anything yet?" asked Chris, as Larry cleaned up the lab area in the morgue. The skull and what was left of Brother John's body lay under a sterile cloth on the table.

"Blunt force trauma to the left side of the skull," said Larry. "Small object. Not something like a baseball bat, something small and very hard. Other than that, he was in damn good shape."

"Small object like ah...like a rock?" inquired Matt.

Larry looked directly at him and said, "yes, like a rock."

~

Matt and Joe were at the station when Joe said, "well, I think it's about time to see Nathan."

"Yup," said Matt, "I agree. He'd be home now and if it's Garrett, no one is safe, especially him or his men."

Driving down muddy roads on the outskirts of Emeryville was a thing that most of the policemen took for granted. Nathan's house was situated on a hill off a dirt road that was usually passable only in one season: the dry one. It was situated across the street from Dennis the lawyer.

"Why in the hell does Dennis want to live way out here," mused Joe.

"He likes the peace and quiet after a day in court and besides his wife likes horses and has some of her own."

They drove past Nathan's sawmill and the truck barns, negotiated past huge piles of planed lumber and mountains of logs.

Bottoming the cruiser out several times, they finally made it to the log cabin. Nathan's wife answered the door and after seating them at the kitchen table and offering coffee, she informed them that her husband was just finishing up a logging contract and would be right there. After a few minutes, Nathan appeared. "What's up?" he asked as he took a seat.

"Well, you know about the most recent event in town?" asked Matt.

"Yeah, that poor guy," he said. "I gave him a ride once. He smelled awful, and it was winter, but I figured it was the least I could do."

"When?" asked Joe.

"Just before he went and did that thing at the tavern. Just before the guys beat 'em up. Unnecessary if you ask me, but who's to say."

"Not after?" asked Matt.

"No," came the quick reply.

"Who would be driving one of the big log trucks? You or one of the men?" asked Matt.

"Usually, Fred drives the big one and then Ted takes turns with Garry on the smaller ones. But they all drive just depends on the day. We're finishing up so most of the men are already gone. Moving on so to speak, except Fred. He works with me all the time."

"We need a list of all the men who work for you. Social security numbers and driver's licenses," said Chris.

"That's easy," said Nathan. "It's all here in the file. I'll get you copies."

"Incidentally," asked Matt, "would you know who would be driving the truck past the old Miller Place on thirty-three, say... in the last three weeks?"

"Well, let's see, that would be on the way to Borchert's and not Whiteman's or Stannard's. It depends on what we cut and what the market wants. Borchert's is usually fir and pine, some spruce. The softwoods." Nathan was deep in thought. "That definitely wouldn't be Fred, so that leaves Garry or Ted."

"I know Fred," said Joe, "but who are Ted and Garry?"

"Ted Davis and Garry Phelps. Both good workers, reliable, although Garry is somewhat of a loner. He's a little odd, but as long as he works and keeps his nose clean, he could have green skin for all I care."

Nathan got up and headed for a small office at the side of the large living room. He turned and asked, "What's with my men?"

"Just a hunch," said Matt. "Not a word of this to anyone."

Chapter Sixty

He watched from the woods. He knew every area of town. Sundays were his time, time to explore, time to bide his time and wait. The more he waited, the more serene and peaceful he became and the more time he had for planning.

~

Dottie reined the horse in. He snorted. "Oh Ferd," she said "just a little farther. You know you're getting too fat." They were in the back of Tom's junkyard and had entered the woods. She wanted to go into the area where Nathan and his crew were cutting wood for a state logging contract. The trails there were wide and sandy in spots and made for a nice, fast ride, where Dottie could feel the wind in her hair and the power of the horse under her. Dottie loved to ride, especially alone. It gave her time to think, although that was usually the moment Ferd would surprise her and bolt or do something stupid. He was a good horse and had managed several times to unseat her, but he always stood close by to make sure she wasn't hurt. She would usually scold him, give him a big pat and then they would continue their ride.

Dottie knew that when this killer was caught and the events of the last weeks were all over, she would have to go and face the music in Alabama. *"Was Bowmaker dead? Did she kill him that night? What happened to her daughters?* All these questions and no answers," she mused.

As she rocketed into a wide turn at a full gallop, she noticed a man on the path several hundred yards ahead of her. She slowed Ferd to a lively trot and then into a walk. The man was looking at several trees in the lot that surrounded a patch of clear-cutting. He looked out of place. It wasn't his clothes or his looks, just his aura, and his manners. As they walked by, she chanced to glance down into his eyes and chills ran down her spine. The eyes staring back at her were dark, menacing, and malevolent. As they passed him she could feel a tenseness in the horse that wasn't there before. Ferd shook his head, snorted and glanced back. "You feel it too, don't ya?" she said as she patted his muscled neck and they continued their ride.

~

Matt stood on the sidewalk, his back to the woods that faced Dottie's barn from across the narrow road. Cold, icy fingers crawled up his back and spine as he glanced behind him.

"He's close," said Dave, "I can feel him."

"Me too," said Matt with a sigh. "I just wonder how all of this will play out?"

They were finishing installing video cameras and adjusting the motion lighting at Eugenia and Dottie's homes. Dottie was the first to complain about them always turning on whenever the wind blew, or a deer or coyote came calling.

"I'll just have to realign them in a few days, is all," Matt told her.

"How's Eugenia doing?" asked Dave casually.

"She's scared," came the reply.

Chapter Sixty-One

Dottie crept silently into the barn. It was dark and as she switched on the light there was a rustling in the straw. *Not a horse,* she thought. She picked up the baseball bat that always leaned near the front sliding door and gripped it tightly.

"Should've called Matt," she muttered.

The camera had clearly shown an intruder. Outside the warm interior of the barn, the wind blew in gusts and the April rain hit the tin roof crescendoing into a dull roar which could be deafening. Friendly neighs sounded from the interior as sleepy-eyed horses shifted in their stalls. There were snorts from the school horses standing in their straight stalls at the far end of the long barn. Ferd whinnied and was answered by Valerie. Ferd had a comfortable box stall while Valerie was relegated to a straight stall at the end of the barn. Ferd and Valerie, the partners in mischief, had to be separated most of the time or trouble became a reality.

There was that rustling sound again. She looked into Ferd's stall and saw Louis, cowering in one corner and a smaller boy held in his arms. Ferd stood guard over them.

Dottie hastily unlatched the stall door and entered. Ferd snorted.

"Oh, shut up," she said. She knelt in the straw, it's sweet smell relaxing her.

"Are you ok?" she said, her hand touching Louis's. "Hiding again?" she asked.

Louis nodded.

"Ok, let's go inside and I'll call Matt and tell 'em where you are."

"Matt's at my house along with Joe," whispered Louis.

"I see," she said.

"Real bad this time. They took gran to the hospital...but mom," he sighed. "I grabbed Lucas and ran. I hope one of my older sisters beat the crap out of him, but that's too much to ask. Why does she let him back in? Why? Kill 'em, just kill 'em," he said angrily.

"No, your mom has to grow balls and stand up to your father. No amount of court orders or legal papers is goin' to take the place of her asserting herself. She has to fight back. She has to press charges and make them stick. She has to fight because she always will be the target as long as he lives because he knows he can get away with it. Lets's go, I have spare beds. Want some cookies and milk?"

Louis nodded his head, "Yes ma'am," he said quietly.

Lucas looked up at her with his large brown eyes and smiled.

The three of them walked out of the barn and into a windy night. As she turned off the lights, she wondered how many more children in situations just like this were out there. But she knew from her own experiences there had to be plenty. Now that many states were starting to acknowledge spousal abuse and domestic violence she wondered if it would make a difference at all. Being aware of it and doing something about it were two different things. Sometimes one had to take matters into their own hands.

Dottie glanced back at the interior of the barn. She felt strange and Ferd looked nervous and uncomfortable.

She didn't see the piercing eyes boring into her back as she left, but she felt them. These were eyes full of hatred. The eyes of a predator looking from his vantage point in the hayloft over the horse stalls. Hidden behind sweet-smelling, alfalfa hay.

Dottie called Matt but got the dispatcher. She told him she had the two boys and they would be sleeping at her house for the night.

~

The following morning Matt sat in Dottie's kitchen.

"Social services are there. The mom is ok, badly bruised, a few broken bones. The grandmother suffered a heart attack but is stable."

"What about the asshole?" asked Dottie, sarcastically.

"In the hospital with severe bruising, two smashed kneecaps and a massive concussion. Unconscious. If he dies, we could have a problem. The mom could be charged with second-degree murder, maybe manslaughter."

"Let's hope he dies and then we could get a huge defense fund going for her defense." After a moment she said, "I'm sorry for talking that way; I don't want anyone to die. It's just that that jerk deserves it."

They sat at the table, Dottie silently sipping her tea and Matt his coffee. Matt reached for a scone, cut it in half, buttered it and smeared the orange marmalade on top. It was the coarse marmalade from Ireland with the large chunks of peel, just the way he liked it. He went for the fresh whipped cream and placed a small spoonful onto the top of the delectable concoction. He sat there smiling at it for a moment and then looked at Dottie, thoughtfully.

She sighed, "Ya see, something inside just snaps and the violence that ensues...you can't stop. It's as if all those wrongs, that have been stored up after years of abuse, have been let loose and they all want to get a crack at the abuser. But, and here's the clincher, how many women get rid of one abuser and go right back into the same situation with another?"

"That's why I never bothered to seek out another partner, for I wasn't sure I could trust myself to not get into another situation like the one I left. It's a form of addiction. I call it guilt because you've been taught that you're unworthy. What a bunch of crap," she said disgustedly.

Matt listened intently, for he knew that he was listening to Dottie's story and, to some extent, his own story.

"There is always that final moment, where you don't care what happens to you. This is why there are so many homicides in the guise of domestic violence. There can only be one winner. Win or lose, both parties have to give it their all in that final conflict. They both realize that there will be others they can prey upon or will prey upon them. Sick isn't it? And when children are involved, the problem escalates as the males learn violent skills and the females learn submissive skills. Bullshit," she said slamming her fist on the table.

"The final straw for me was when he sold our girls. Sold them for a profit. I still see his sneering face. He knew that that night was the final showdown and he was prepared to kill me, but I beat him to it. To this day, I don't know where my girls are or even if they're still alive."

Matt stared at her, never had he heard something so vile as selling your children.

"How old were they?" he asked, quietly.

"Three and four. Blonde hair, hazel eyes, cute little girls. Something a pedophile would drool over." She hesitated, "sorry, don't mean to go there."

She continued, "I hope they went fast if they were murdered. If they, by the grace of God, are still alive, I hope that they had good lives and they were kept together. That's all I can pray for. As far as seeing them again, I've lost all hope for that a long time ago."

After a few moments, Dottie said, "Well, time for the boys to go back. If they need a place tonight, I'm here."

There were sounds of feet on the stairs and two figures appeared at the doorway.

"Fresh orange juice," said Dottie, "and how about some scones?"

Matt turned and headed down the back steps of Dottie's house. The boys were already at the door of the police car arguing about who would be in the front seat.

"One last thing," she called, as Matt stepped from the porch and proceeded to the cruiser.

Matt stopped and turned to face her. Their eyes locked.

"What goes on behind closed doors, is what we feed our kids."

Matt nodded his head, smiled thoughtfully, turned and headed to the car.

Chapter Sixty-Two

"What the hell is that?" asked Steve, now propped up on one elbow. The clock at the side of the bed read 3:30 am.

Larry rolled over and said, "Wha?" sleepily.

"That noise, like a scraping sound. Now I hear a horse; I think. Oh no, not Valerie again! This is beginning to be a nightmare," wailed Steve.

From the blackness of the yard, Steve heard Dave's voice say, "what is it, girl?"

Steve bolted down the back stairs. He was in his underwear and bare feet. Howie was close behind him, bumping and bouncing down the steep incline and voicing his displeasure at this rude interruption.

As Steve unbolted the back door, he heard Dave's voice shout sternly, "Stop or I'll shoot."

Dave was at the wood line of the yard intently looking into the woods, Valerie beside him. Momentarily a silence descended and then scurrying and the breaking of branches ensued. Valerie snorted and started into the woods.

"No girl," said Dave, placing his hand on her shoulder. She stopped, sensing something not right. She arched her neck and snorted.

Steve, running out the back door found both of them looking into the woods. Valerie glanced at him and looked back at the woods.

"Intruder," said Dave.

"Valerie, right?" said Steve.

"I don't think so. We both heard footsteps, that's when all hell broke loose. In the morning we'll get a team over here, first light."

Nedo emerged from the carriage house. He had on shorts and a tee-shirt. "What in Hell?" he said, eyeing the horse.

"Our new guard dog," said Dave.

"Ya think he was here?" said Nedo, quietly.

Dave nodded. "Running feet through the underbrush, motion lights on. I heard a scraping sound first and then light footfalls on that new patch of gravel we just put down under that eave. I heard a curse and I got out of bed. Grabbed my gun, but Valerie here beat me to it."

"You sure it wasn't her?" Nedo inquired.

"No. It was human."

"This has to stop," pronounced Larry, coming out the back door of the house. He had on a pair of pajamas and a sweater. "It's the middle of the frigging night."

"I could tie her to the back door like a guard horse," said Steve, sheepishly, "or let her roam around the yard."

Larry glared at him. "And the next thing you'll want to do is take her in bed with you."

Dave smiled at the interaction between the two men, sighed and said, "time to wake up Dottie." He speed-dialed her number.

When she arrived, Dottie found the men patting, rubbing and scratching Valerie, who was in her glory.

"I can't figure how she got out," Dottie mused. " She must have sensed something wrong. Unless little Laura didn't tie her in her stall securely. She was the last one with her yesterday."

"Well, she saved the day," said Nedo.

"We don't need a guard dog, we have Valerie here," laughed Dave.

Throwing his hands in the air, Larry shouted, "Hell why not the entire damned stable?" and turned to go back into the house.

~

The next morning forensics had the area corded off. A shoe print was found just outside the backdoor of the carriage house. Dave and the men looked around the yard for other clues.

A rock, rounded and able to fit nicely within a man's hand was found lying innocently on the seat of the chair that Dave had been sitting in the night before. When Dave saw the rock he understood several things; that Garrett knew who he was and that he would stop at nothing to kill him.

"It's as if he's saying, it's me, come and get me if you can. This is a real change in his pattern. This is a taunt. To my knowledge, he's never done that before. Usually, it's the element of surprise, but this time it's different," Dave told Nedo.

Lydia and Olivia watched the operations from the back porch of Steve and Larry's house. Steve, who did most of the cooking for the couple, had made the lemonade. Olivia didn't like lemonade, but when she tasted the fresh-squeezed version, it changed her mind.

"What's in this lemonade?" Lydia asked.

"I always put fresh lavender in it. Makes for a nice taste," replied Steve. "But you have to be very careful with lavender. If you are using the oil, you have to use it very, very sparingly. Same way with mint."

"I like it," said Olivia.

Differently Double

Chapter Sixty-Three

It had been a busy and intense day at the police station. The business at Larry's house and the searching, along with regular police duties, kept everyone at the station busy. An all-points had been posted for one Garrett Sellers, aka Garry Phelps. As his employment at the logging company had ended several days previously, the urgency of finding Garrett had increased exponentially. So far, his skills in the woods and survival techniques had benefitted him greatly, as the FBI and local law enforcement had lost him yet again.

Matt knew deep down that he wouldn't leave unless he, Gene and Dave were dead. And who else? He shivered as he thought about the ones he loved and cared deeply for.

"Hell," he muttered, "no one's safe."

Matt closed the door of the patrol car and walked toward the porch steps at the rear of his house. It was a small porch, enclosed with glass windows, but it kept the wind from entering the kitchen in the colder months of the year. He glanced at the garage and then into the backyard. The woods were darkening in the late afternoon shadows. He sensed it rather than saw it; something, someone lurking there. Watching, waiting.

Then he saw her; little Selma. She quietly looked at him and smiled. He turned from the steps and walking past the garage he made his way into the yard in the direction of where she stood. The grass was greening. Soon he'd have mowing to do and Karen would be tending her flower garden.

He didn't see him at first, he heard him; sensed him. Selma screamed at him. Hearing the message in his head, "watch out!" Matt turned just in time to duck from the blow of the rock held high in Garrett's hand. Matt grabbed for his arm and twisted it. Garrett grunted. This man had strength, but Matt had tactical fighting experience. The blow from Matt's fist sent his assailant backward against a small swing set, the metal frame rocking as he hit it with his back. Garrett rushed him again and this time Matt was ready for him. Matt swung his arm up to make sure his head avoided connecting with the rock held in Garrett's hand. The rock made an impact with his wrist instead and Matt felt his bone snap. He raised his leg to divert the force from the rest of his attacker's body. Matt kicked outward and his foot connected with the soft, fleshy part just below Garrett's groin. Garrett stumbled backward. He kept himself upright, the rock still held in his hand. He momentarily stopped and stared at Matt. Twenty feet separated them.

"You abandoned me," he sneered.

"Is that what this shit's all about?" Matt gasped. "You bastard."

A crow called from the confines of the woods and Matt's eyes, temporarily adverted, saw the small, limp body hanging from the lowest branch of the crab apple tree just visible over Garrett's shoulder. Matt momentarily froze.

"No," he screamed, "no!" and then Matt charged him with all his pent-up fury and anger. Garrett was taken by surprise. Never had he seen such rage in another man, other than his father when he was young. Fear suddenly displaced Garrett's rage and hatred. He flung the rock down, turned and ran into the woods. He would not stop running until his fears left and the demon had possession of him again.

~

Matt held onto the pole of the swing-set gasping. His wrist hurt like hell and it was limp and starting to swell.

Karen was running toward him, "Oh my God," she screamed. "I called 911. I saw most of it, but it happened so quickly." She hugged him tightly. He smiled down at her and kissed the top of her head.

"Is he gone?"

"I think I scared the shit outta him." He gasped. "I think this was the first time, except for his father, that he wasn't in control. I never saw him afraid, totally afraid before."

He stroked his wife's cheek.

"I just lost it. I became Bradley," he said quietly. "And Dottie, I remember what Dottie said about losing it. The rage possesses you and no amount of training can control it."

"It's human nature," Karen said quietly, looking up into his tired face.

"Your arm," she said, taking his arm in both her hands. "It's broken, I'll bet my life on it. It looks like the wrist. Let's go in."

They held onto each other and made their way toward the house amidst the fire siren and the sounds of running feet on the sidewalk. Matt was covered in sweat, his clean uniform streaked with mud and grass. He met the ambulance crew as he approached the porch.

Aaron, head of the emergency squad, ran to him. "You ok buddy?" Aaron asked.

"Little beat up and my heart won't stop racing, but I'm ok.," said Matt.

"His wrist is broken," said Karen quietly.

"Let's go inside, I'll feel better when I can sit down," said Matt.

Police cars, lights flashing, pulled up to the small house.

Steve and Larry were running down the sidewalk. Larry, out of breath, arrived just as Matt was being helped up the stairs.

Nedo squirmed his way into the crowd. "You ok, Matt?" he said over the din.

"Yeah. Go to the back yard," Matt said, facing the small group. "Whatever you do, don't let Lydia or any of the kids see what's hanging from the tree."

Dave arrived and hearing this he turned on his flashlight and made his way into the small backyard that bordered the woods. Nedo followed him.

Policemen immediately put up barriers, blocking the way of the curiosity seekers.

Differently Double

Chapter Sixty-Four

"This is sick," sneered Nedo. "Get pics and then cut it down."

"Typical Garrett," said Dave.

"We're checking the woods," said one of the men, "but he's long gone."

"I'll bet he's still running. I really liked that cat. Dammit," said Dave, absently.

"He had to make a statement somehow. Hey it's me!" said Nedo. "The bastard."

"Need me?" asked Larry, making his way into the backyard. Larry looked at the body of Spyder, Lydia's cat. Approaching it, he turned it with his hand. The body was illuminated by the beams of several flashlights.

"I don't give a shit if it's a dog, a human or a parakeet, it's still the same thing; killing. Unnecessary. I hate abuse and I see enough of it at the morgue," he muttered. "Sometimes I just wanna take the parents, spouse or whoever the hell they are and do the same thing to them. But then I think, I bet this is what's been done to them. It's normal for them. Sick isn't it?" he sneered as he faced the men.

Larry sighed and stood there stroking Spyder's soft fur. Matted blood congealed from one ear and her face was distorted into a form of grimace, exposing upper canines. Then, he said absently, "Blunt force trauma. The skull's caved in. It was quick. She didn't suffer." He turned and walked several steps and then turned to face them. He said, "wanna report? I'll write one."

Nedo looked from him and then back to the cat. "Why not," he said.

Larry nodded, turned and walked out of the yard.

~

Aaron looked at Matt's wrist. "We're stabilizing this and to the hospital, you go."

Matt frowned.

"No excuses," Aaron said, standing his ground. "You wanna be able to shoot again, right?"

Matt glared at him. "It's my gun arm," he muttered.

"Boy, he really must've slammed you," said one of the EMTs.

"Yeah, just think if it was my head. He was aiming for my head and he missed," said Matt.

"You wouldn't be here right now if he didn't," said Marty, the fire chief. "Christ, it's swollen."

"Looks like we gotta Colles' fracture and maybe some displacement in there too. Let's stabilize and roll," said Aaron. "Hospital's a-waitin'."

Matt looked at his wife and sighed.

"I'll stay here until Eugenia gets here," she said.

At that moment Eugenia entered the kitchen. "Go," she said, "I know about the backyard, now go."

"How do you know?" said Karen.

"I was just briefed, now go," she shouted sternly.

~

Chris came up to Nedo and said, "I'm putting a man here tonight. I don't think he'll be back, but who the hell knows. We have an extra patrol on the other end of the village. Lydia will be coming momentarily. Josh said he'll make sure she gets home safely from his house."

Nedo nodded and said, "we're headed for the hospital. We need to brief him. I think our Mr. Matt will be out of commission for a while."

Chris nodded his head in agreement.

"We're rolling," said Aaron. Aaron's brother, also a squad member, jumped into the waiting ambulance.

Chapter Sixty-Five

"Seven minutes flat, not bad," remarked Dave as they parked their car at the hospital. They approached the emergency room entrance just as Matt was wheeled in.

"I had trouble keeping up with them, especially on those roads," remarked Nedo. "No wonder people complain about that road. Dark as hell and all those deer."

~

They were waiting for x-rays to be done and the IV Team to complete their tasks when Aaron came up to them and said, "It's a bad fracture. Several bones, so I'm guessing he'll be in surgery for a while. They're assembling a team right now for the operation."

"That fast?" said Dave.

Aaron nodded and told them, "they'll be coming for him in a few minutes. You won't have long for your interview. He's a bit groggy but give it a try. We've gotta get back."

~

Dave and Nedo sat in chairs at the side of Matt's bed. Karen had gone to the cafeteria to get herself a cup of tea and coffee for the two men.

Karen entered the room and sat on the opposite side of the bed. Her cell phone rang. It was Eugenia informing her that Lydia was home with her and that she had told her what happened. Lydia wanted to see her father but was told no, not until the operation was over. She was to get a good night's sleep. Karen would be home as soon as she knew everything was ok.

Matt looked subdued and thoughtful. "He's blaming me for abandoning him. That's it. We had a brief talk, very brief. That's what this shit's all about; abandonment."

He continued, "I bet his life was no picnic after I left. I now know what Dottie said to me is true. There's just so much a human can take before they break. When I saw the cat, that's when I lost it. That's when I got this renewed strength deep inside me that said *kill him*."

Matt suddenly brightened. "Oh my God," he said, awe in his voice. "I went into the backyard because I saw Selma. She was standing there smiling at me. I was going into the house and when I spotted her, I went back to see her."

Dave's mouth suddenly turned dry.

"The last crime scene, the one in Pennsylvania, the pictures. Wasn't that Selma near the three people who were killed? She's following him!" Matt said in awe.

"Remember, she said she was going to help," said Dave, quietly.

"She alerted me he was there. I heard 'Watch out.' That's when I turned and lifted my arm. He was already on me. I would've been dead if it hadn't been for her," Matt said.

Nedo just looked at both men and shook his head.

"Yes, Brian, please put it in the report," said Dave.

"It's gonna be your ass, not mine," Nedo said to Dave. "What do I call it?" he said sarcastically. "Girl ghost, spirit, a helper from beyond? Just what do I call it?"

"How about a little girl named Selma," said Dave quietly.

Chapter Sixty-Six

Gene was fishing off the dock at the Fish and Game pond. It was mid-morning on his day off. Before he got back to the necessary things he needed to do, like weeding his garden, he thought he would just fish a little and maybe catch his dinner. He didn't see Garrett, but he felt him. That feeling that washed over him the day in the cafe, now assailed all his senses. Sitting on the edge of the dock, he looked around nervously and stood.

He cautiously walked to the beginning of the dock, but he saw no one. He scanned the field and the area around the clubhouse, the indoor and outdoor shooting ranges and the trap and skeet range. No one. He shrugged his shoulders, but the feeling persisted.

Gene headed for the path through the woods that would lead him through the field in the back of his home and the antique shop. Dappled sunlight shadowed the path, birds chirped noisily and the occasional whir of insect wings gave way to the occasional whine of breeze in the boughs of the spruce trees.

Gene kept looking over his shoulder and to the right and left along the trail. Something was wrong: he knew it. Someone was watching him. He walked a little faster. The last thing he wanted was to encounter his murderous brother. What would he do? All his senses were alerted as little wood creatures made tiny skittering noises in the undergrowth.

He didn't see the man that crouched behind the trunk of a large cherry tree at the side of the path until it was too late.

He heard a twig snap and a footfall, but before he could turn around, he felt a jarring sensation at the back of his head accompanied by a hollow ringing sound. Passing into blackness, he fell in a heap at the side of a large rock.

Gene drifted in and out of consciousness. Little snippets of life assailing his senses. He was aware of the coppery smell of blood, the ache at the back of his skull, the blurriness of his vision and the wet, sticky feel of blood down his back when he tried to move his shoulder. *Don't move* is what his mind was telling him, *just don't move.* And so, he didn't.

Garrett dragged Gene's body to a place behind the large rock. Momentarily conscious Gene heard a voice. The voice sounded hollow and far off. "Well, well, brother dear, finally we meet again. I'm saving you till last. Then I can carefully take my time killing you."

Slightly out of breath, Garrett straightened and found himself looking straight into the inquiring eyes of Mandy, who stood quietly by. It must have taken every bit of courage for her to be here for she was visibly trembling.

Her head was cocked to one side and looking up at Garrett, she said boldly, "hullo Dark Man. What have you done to Mr. Gene?"

Mandy liked Gene; he was nice to her. When she visited him at the antique shop with her mother, he always gave her some little figurine or trinket. He always told her how pretty she looked.

She became very agitated as Garrett grabbed her hand, yanking her to one side and off-balance so that she fell onto her knees and then rolled.

"Get up," he sneered.

She clumsily got to her feet and ran toward him, enraged. Her fists were clenched and flailing. He grabbed for her again and this time he managed to grip her arm painfully. But, no matter how hard he gripped her, she did not call out. Her resolve was amazing.

Garrett momentarily glanced back at the rock where the body of his brother lay. "What the hell?" he muttered as shapes began to form deep in the woods and around the body. The little girl in the sundress was the most visible. She stood in front of the group, hands on her hips and looking directly at him. The figures surrounding her looked somewhat familiar to him in an uncanny way. He knew in his mind they were all dead. Were they coming for him?

Garrett had dropped Mandy's hand as he turned and saw the apparitions. Mandy had a moment to recover and give Garret a resounding kick in the ankle.

"Shit," he roared.

Grabbing her by the arm he pulled her toward him and whispered hoarsely in her ear, "Let's go girly, we have a job to do." He pulled her to the side and gripping her hand he began to run with her toward the woods.

Differently Double

Chapter Sixty-Seven

"I can't find her," Ginger shouted into the phone. "She was playing with some rocks in the backyard. She was waiting for me to fix a snack. Now she's gone. Just like that."

"Ok, calm down," said Chris. He had just answered his phone at the police station and was listening intently.

He slammed down the receiver.

"Ah, shit," he barked. "Let's go. Mandy's missing. They can't find her."

"What if he's got her?" remarked one of the men.

Nedo, who had just entered the room, said, "Yeah, we were out again early this morning. That bastard just disappeared into the woods back of the swamp. No telling where he's gone."

The fire whistle blew as home scanners told of the news of a missing child. Firemen and EMT crews assembled to await further orders for a search and rescue.

"After all, Mandy's been onto Garrett for some time. She knew who he was before we did," commented Chris.

Nedo nodded.

Teams formed and fanned out in many directions in search of the missing little girl with Down syndrome.

Differently Double

Chapter Sixty-Eight

Mandy sat facing Garrett. He broke off a piece of sandwich and gave it to her.

"Why are you mean?" she questioned. "I see a nice man then see a bad man."

Garrett didn't understand at first. Then he started to get the idea of what she was talking about.

"This evil has been in me a long time and now it's time for me to go. But before I go, I have to right some wrongs that were done to me. People abandoned me. They let me down. Didn't take me with them. They'll pay for that," he said with conviction.

She looked over his shoulder and remarked, "the little girl, she love you. Always love you. It's very sad. I'm sad," she mumbled. Her face was stained with sweat and her little legs were bleeding from the thorns they had run through.

She continued, "Why you do bad things to people? Why you let something make you?"

Garrett was now agitated, but not agitated enough to kill her. Not just yet anyway.

"Lots of people coming. Terd is coming too," she said.

He glared at her.

"I like the nice lady with you. She loves you. She has nice hair...looks like you," she mumbled.

Mandy was quiet for a time and then began to hum a song. "Save us Terd...,"

"Shut up," Garrett shouted, "just shut the hell up."

Mandy looked at him, large tears welling in her eyes. "Girl says me be not fraid. Girl will help me."

"Why, oh why, did I have to bring you? I can kill those three and then leave. I'll be a free man."

"Yes," said Mandy, "Free. No more hurting people."

He looked at her.

"For a cretin, you're pretty smart," he sneered.

Mandy felt it at first. It was an intensifying of the energy around her, almost like an electrical charge. She looked around and she shivered. It was midday, but suddenly the air took on a density as though it was dusk before a thunderstorm.

Garret stood. "Time to go," he said brusquely as he yanked her to standing and began dragging her in the direction of the woods. Something spurred him on, something dark and evil.

Making the shelter of the fence line, he dragged Mandy up a small slope and onto a well-worn path. It led to the far backfields of the Vesley farm, a neighboring farm on the other side of the Fish and Game Club. Dragging Mandy through a small stream, he kept going. The path led upward and the dark shadows of the woods sheltered them from sight.

"Hey mister, mister dark man, you weren't dark back there when we were sitting there...mister dark man," she gasped.

"Oh, for Christ's sake, shut up will ya," he said. They were now standing at the edge of a large, grassy clearing on the top of a high hill.

"I tired," she said.

"Let's go. I wanna make it as far outta here as we can. I'll get rid of you and circle back. I can get this job done by tomorrow morning."

He and Mandy ran into the grassy meadow. Something was urging her on, something she didn't quite understand, but it felt safe.

"You need me," she blurted out.

He stopped and stared at her. He was breathing hard. Mandy's breath was coming in short gasps, but she still was able to run.

"I need you?" he said. "What the hell do I need you for? I'm gonna kill you," he sneered bending to look her straight in the eyes.

"No," said Mandy, "they won't let you."

"They? Who the hell are they?"

At that moment, Mandy collapsed. She fell face forward.

Garrett extracted a large rock from his pocket. "No better time than now," he muttered.

He grabbed for a piece of the child's hair and yanked her face up. He was standing over her, straddling her small, plump body when someone shouted at him. It was a child's voice, but forceful, authoritative..."No."

He let go of her hair and Mandy's face dropped into the tangle of grass and vetch where she lay. As he straightened, he saw the dark shadow. It came from within him and now it was fully visible just in front of his body. It had no features just undulating, dark, raw energy. It moved away from him stealthily, silently and then it turned to face him.

Selma suddenly appeared and faced the shadow. She had her back to Garrett. Her little hands were on her hips and she looked straight at the dark entity. Garrett saw thousands of spirits surrounding them; an army of light and shadows. There was no sound, even the birds stopped chirping. It was as if they were standing in a complete vacuum.

~

Terrified, Garrett stumbled backward, away from the scene before him. A little girl, transparent and shimmering with an unGodly light, hands on her hips in command and hundreds of shadows, some dark and others shimmering with light. They all were circling. Circling around and round as if at any moment they would pounce on the dark figure standing in front of the tiny girl.

He didn't see or hear the galloping horse descending upon him until it was too late. Ferd squealed and knocked him down, but Garrett rolled and uprighted himself, and sprinted in the opposite direction. The horse descended on him again and this time bared his teeth to bite him. Garrett extended his arm with the rock clutched into the palm of his hand. With all his strength, he hit the horse full in its quivering mouth. Garrett spun around and headed back toward Mandy, who was lying dazed in the grass.

Ferd squealed, shook his head, spun around and took off after the man. He intersected Garrett and with one rear hoof managed to hit him squarely in the upper arm. Garrett, momentarily knocked off balance, collapsed and rolled. With the rock still held in his hand, he scrambled to his feet just as Father and Eugenia emerged from the path in the woods.

They saw the battle between the dark entity and the light spirits. The spirits were waiting to take this dark force home. Father, gasping, stopped. Catching his breath he said one of his prayers, a prayer aimed at freeing a soul of darkness; a Releasing Prayer. The prayer would help the dark soul make its way home, back to the loving arms of God.

They watched spellbound as the dark figure seemed to be pulling apart like taffy in the hands of an expert confectioner. And then, in a flash, it was gone. The only figure standing was that of a small child in a sundress.

~

Valerie, with Dottie riding bareback and hanging on for dear life, arrived in the large clearing and galloped toward her buddy, Ferd. Not to be outdone, she extended her head, flattened her ears and with her teeth bared she charged Garrett. Dottie, gripping the horse's sides tighter, grabbed for another hunk of mane and held on for dear life. Valerie bit into Garrett's opposite shoulder and spun him around.

Garrett, reeling from her assault was now fully exposed. One last kick from Ferd landed in the center of Garrett's chest and sent him flying backward.

Garrett landed with a thud. Blood gushed from his mouth and the front of his shirt was beginning to darken.

Differently Double

Chapter Sixty-Nine

Selma bent over the prone body of Mandy. Mandy, somewhat disoriented, sat up. Mandy smiled at the luminous, transparent figure of the little girl. Father saw another figure beside Selma, that of a slight woman, a woman who now had her hand extended to Selma. He heard the woman say gently to her daughter, "she'll be fine. You're not needed here anymore. We must go home."

Father smiled, "Go with God," he whispered and he saw Selma take the hand of her mother and walk quietly toward the woods in the afternoon sunlight.

~

Lydia, Olivia, Josh, Alex, and Dave arrived breathless followed shortly by Nedo and half the town. In the midst of them was Gene. Lou, the mayor, had found him sitting at the base of a rock along the trail and had assisted him to his feet. Gene was going after his brother no matter what. After a few terse words with Lou, Chris, who was following Lou, grabbed one of Gene's arms. Lou grabbed Gene's other arm and they struggled up the path toward the commotion in the field.

Nedo stood by the prone body of Garrett, as Mandy made her way toward them. Nedo glanced up in time to see the mother and daughter slowly making their way toward the nearby woods where a bright spot of light was getting larger and larger. They shimmered and were transparent, but he could still make them out as two people, one a little girl in a sundress and the other an older woman from another time.

Nedo's skin was on fire and he shivered. "I'm getting too old for this shit," he muttered.

Dave, half running, almost caught up to the two retreating figures making their final way home. They both turned and smiled at him. "Go back," he heard them whisper, "you have more to do," and then they turned and were instantly swallowed up by the light. Eugenia caught up to Dave who was now rooted to the spot. He was crying openly, huge gasps of breath coming from his throat. She put her arms around him and held him as he let go of all the years of hate, anger, and misery.

~

Mandy quietly knelt beside Garrett and whispered, "You'll be ok now. Bad man gone. The nice lady here. Wants to take you with her."

His eyes slowly focused on Mandy.

Dottie, sliding down from Valerie's back, stood quietly behind Nedo and next to Charlie, Mandy's father. Charlie was shaking violently as he stood there. The brevity of the situation playing out before him was more than he thought he could handle. He marveled at his daughter and tears came to his eyes.

Dottie placed her hand on Charlie's arm and smiled at him.

~

Blood oozed from the wound in Garret's chest, his breathing was labored and his eyes weren't focusing as they should. He looked in the direction of Mandy's voice and when Ferd snorted; he tensed. He couldn't move. Nothing in his body wanted to move.

Garrett saw snippets of memories, events that had happened long, long ago. He and his father catching fish in the bayou; his father and mother teaching him to ride a bike when he was very small. Happy times. Times he had forgotten. Times erased from his memory; until now.

Kneeling beside Garrett, Gene reached for Garrett's hand and held it. Garrett looked up at his brother and smiled faintly.

Father knelt near Garrett's head and anointed his forehead with something that felt slippery, like oil. Garrett felt a calmness he never felt before wash over him as light filled the darkest places in his soul.

He averted his gaze and smiling up at Father he gasped, "Guess I'm going straight to hell, right?"

"No," said Father quietly. "If you have the courage, und I know you do, you'll take the hand of the angel und whoever else is here for you, und go to Him. Remember, God loves all his children," said Father, quietly, "you're no exception."

"What about the...the darkness?" Garrett stammered, his chest heaving as he gasped for more air.

"All gone now und the dark places within you are now filled with light. We made sure of that."

Ferd snorted and Garrett's body gave a violent twitch.

"He's agreeing with us. He senses the difference too," said Gene, quietly.

"I'm really a fu-fuckin screwup, aren't I," whispered Garrett, blood running from his mouth. He looked into the eyes of his brother.

A gurgling sound could be heard deep within his chest. Still looking at his brother, he gave a short gasp, his head slumped to the side and all labored breathing ceased.

A woman, transparent and barely visible, knelt beside Garrett. Taking Garrett's hand, she looked directly at Dottie. Dottie recognized her sister and started to weep. Gene smiled and looked at the translucent figure of his mother with wonder, "All is forgiven," he whispered. "Love you, Mom."

"He's going with me," the spirit said in a voice that sounded sweet and gentle to their ears. It was like a whispering breeze. "We have many things to do." Suddenly the area where they were became very bright and Garrett's spirit, rising out of his prone body, joined the woman. They disappeared with a flash into its brightness.

Ferd snorted and pawed the ground. Dottie put her hand on his silky neck and he nuzzled her arm. She kissed him on his soft muzzle and patted him once more before looking again at the lifeless body of the man who lay in the grass of the clearing.

The sun was beginning to set and vivid colors streaked the sky. The wind started to blow, causing the grass to wave in its wake.

"Guess we're done here," said Father as he rose to his feet.

Mandy was helped up by Gene, who stood over her, holding her hand.

Dottie led Ferd away but not before placing Mandy on his back and telling her to hang on.

A bolt of lightning streaked across the dusky sky.

"Ferd loves lighting and he loves to run in the rain," she said, "so hang on."

Mandy's father came to the other side of the horse and placed his hand on the muscular neck. "Thank you," he whispered to the horse.

Ferd's ears twitched as he acknowledged the man. He sensed that this man belonged to the little girl sitting on his back.

Dottie, grabbing a handful of Valerie's mane, leaped onto her back and grabbed for the lead rope she had attached to Ferd's halter.

Everyone watched as a brilliant flash of lightning lit up the clearing, followed by a rumble of thunder as two horses with their riders galloped toward the edge of the hill into the setting sun.

Chapter Seventy

Dave and Nedo had received a phone call from the prosecutor's office in Mobile, Alabama. A preliminary hearing would commence in three days. Dottie had received legal summons previously and wisely let her attorneys take care of all the particulars. All she had to do when she finally got to Mobile was to tell her story. Other witnesses were being called and maybe, after all these years, justice might be a possibility.

~

It was a bright, sunny day in Mobile as hundreds of people waited for the car bearing Dottie Bowmaker to the federal courthouse for her hearing. Dennis exited the car first followed by Rick Bateman, her defense attorney, and then Dottie. Press reporters shoved cameras and microphones in Dottie's face and shouted questions, but a small group of police suddenly surrounded her and kept order. Inside the courthouse, they made their way down the corridor to the courtroom.

As Dottie walked down the aisle to take her seat next to her attorney and Dennis, she noticed a woman sitting at the edge of the first row of seats. The woman turned and faced her. Dottie recognized her immediately. The woman rose and with tears streaming down her face, she embraced Dottie. Sandy Elliot was as gracious as she remembered her. Her steel-grey hair was trimmed short and her slight frame was draped in a casual pants suit of charcoal grey. A silken, mauve-pink blouse peeked out from the top of the ensemble. Her face was lined and showed a life well lived with happiness and contentment. Her blue eyes sparkled with delight at seeing her long lost friend again.

Dottie's eyes momentarily glanced at Sandy's side and looked at the two young women seated next to her. They looked somewhat familiar. No, impossible, it couldn't be!

Dottie abruptly turned and faced forward, all her breath momentarily taken from her. She was visibly shaking and she started to cry. With all her mother's intuition, she knew these were her girls; her babies. But how? Dottie felt a hand on her sleeve and as she glanced back at Sandy, Sandy winked and smiled at her.

"All stand," said the bailiff as the judge entered the courtroom.

The Honorable Virginia Ouderkirk was a woman who was fair but abrupt and did not broker games of any kind in her courtroom. A rather large woman in her late sixties, she had steel-grey hair and piercing blue eyes that took in everything.

"This is a hearing to access the validity of the prosecution seeking a formal indictment," said the Judge.

Dottie was led to the podium. Her attorney, Rick Bateman, watched as she took the oath and sat down in the witness box.

"Now Dottie," said Craig Ives, the prosecutor, "I need you to relate everything that you remember about the days before and after, and the night that your husband, David Bowmaker, died. Please don't leave anything out. Even the slightest little thing can be important here."

"Please," Craig nodded and Dottie began her story.

"I need to make something very plain here," began Dottie. "I need to give you some background on my marriage to David Bowmaker so you'll understand what happened in the end."

Dottie looked tentatively at the judge who nodded her head.

Dottie continued. "I was an older woman who came from a poor farming family in the south. David was a big shot lawyer. Small man, big ego, that was David. But, where I came from, he was a huge step up. At first, he wanted to show me off, dress me in fancy clothing and take me places. He was an older man, well-seasoned in Mobile society and well connected. We had some nice times and I liked my place in society. About a year into our marriage, I began to realize that David was very manipulative, as well as verbally and psychologically abusive.

It was after our second child was born and the physical abuse started, that I really began to hate the man. But for the life of me, he would always have kind words the next hour and I'd forget it all and off he'd go to the office.

It was during that time I began to notice small things that were out of the ordinary, like the large amounts of cash in suitcases in the spare bedroom closets. Also, certain people would show up for late-night conferences and these people weren't just ordinary people. Some were judges, others lawyers and many were mob members.

So, I began to write down things into a notebook I kept hidden. My little black book, I called it. It was rather a large tome in the end and I hid it very well. I knew if he ever found it, he'd kill me or have me killed," she sighed. "I always had dreams of using it against him, but the odds of that were about zero."

"Excuse me, your honor. I have a question for the witness," said Ives.

The judge nodded her head.

"What happened to the notebook?"

The judge looked at Dottie, but Dottie was undeterred. "I'm getting to that," said Dottie, wearily.

The Judge smiled wanly and nodded her head to continue.

Dottie sighed and said, "Deals he called them. The kidnappings, the hits, the bribes." Dottie paused, she seemed to be reminiscing in her mind. She scowled and then continued her narrative.

"I found out, and don't ask me how, I can't remember, but I found out that he was famous for his bribing. He always had a ready supply of cash. Where he got it, beats me. Don't ask me why I didn't go to the police. Ya see I recognized several members of the police department in that office of his more than once in the course of my sojourn as his wife. So, I knew I couldn't trust anyone. And, I mean no one."

"The mob, the politicians they all came to David to be fixed. Meanwhile, David became more and more abusive, flaunting...maniacal. I loved my girls and would kill to protect them with my dying breath and I was prepared to."

Tired, she spoke slowly and quietly. "I was the one that would make the cash drops and pickups to and from local businesses. It was at this time that I also kept another book, a ledger and that, gentlemen, you have in your possession. Or someone has it. I gave it to Sandy to keep with the files at the office a few days before I ran. I knew the FEDS would be raiding the office sometime, and what better way for them to pick it up."

Both the prosecution and the defense nodded agreement.

Dottie continued. "My friendship with Sandy started one evening when she babysat for me as I had to go to the clinic down the road to have my broken ribs checked and I was seeing double from the results of a concussion. Compliments of David. It was at this time that I began to realize that my home was being watched and the phone lines were tapped.

David was more controlled than he had been and more congenial several days before I left. He had a bad outburst one evening several weeks before, but now he was more controlled and I became paranoid. I kept thinking *this is the end*. He is going to have me killed.

"On the evening of the," she sighed, "event, I had to go and get stitches removed. I also wanted to go to the pharmacy. Sandy was to babysit and I left as soon as she arrived."

The prosecution stood and moved for a question. "Do you remember the time?" Craig Ives asked.

"Don't quote me," said Dottie, "but I think it was around six. I remember I had to walk several blocks to the clinic and, with the waiting time and all, I think I got out of there around eight."

The judge nodded and Dottie continued.

"Sandy was to leave when David got home. Sandy would have already put the girls to bed. I remember walking home and looking all around on the streets and at the parked cars. There were two I thought to be out of place. They gave me the creeps when I walked by them because the men inside were obviously watching me. I remember I had had a conversation with Sandy several weeks before. She told me privately that David told her to get rid of all the files in the office. I wondered if this was indeed the end."

"Anyway," she continued, "I got to the house and I saw no lights. It was all dark, no nightlight in the girls' room upstairs, no hall light, nothing. I opened the door and walked in. I heard a door open and David came out of the living room into the vestibule, where I stood. Now, this vestibule was large...large enough for several huge display cases. It was just inside the front door. This part of the downstairs foyer was used to display all his awards and golf trophies and some expensive figurines he liked to collect.

I stood there. I didn't move. I didn't know what to expect. There was a small lamp in the living room he had lit and its light fell out into the hallway. I could see his face enough to know he was sneering at me.

I remember him telling me, that they were gone, my girls, and that now it was just he and I. He started toward me. The look on his face was murderous; hateful.

Time felt like it stood still for a few moments. The rage crept up to me like a volcano. Finally, after I got my breath back, I screamed at him. I wanted to know how and why?"

She hesitated and then continued, her voice louder. "One thing I will tell you, he was not a bluffer. He told the truth and I had no reason to disbelieve him. When he told me he had sold them, gotten rid of the girls, I believed him. Our girls, I know he hated them, but for the life of me I had no idea why."

Dottie looked straight at the two young women who sat next to Sandy and then at Craig Ives. After several moments, she continued.

"Sold the little crybabies, they're gone now. I made a ton of money off 'em, is what he told me. I called him a bastard and I remember all I wanted to do was kill him. I had nothing left. I grabbed a golf club from the umbrella stand where several were stored. I swung and connected with the glass in one of the cases. As the glass shattered he just looked at me and started to laugh. The second swing connected with the side of his head. I remember hearing bone crack and the incredible look of total surprise, shock on his face. Then his eyes rolled back into his head and he fell forward. He just laid there. I remember little grunts coming from him, like moans. I took one more swing at one of the cases and more glass shattered and then I just stood there. I remember time standing still like everything was in slow motion. I don't even remember dropping the golf club.

I yanked open the bottom drawer of the largest case. There was glass all over. I grabbed the black notebook and shoved it down my sweatshirt. And then I turned, opened the door and I ran... I just ran, and ran," she said, her voice trailing off.

Dottie hung her head. She was crying silently.

After a few moments, the prosecutor stood and questioned Dottie. Did she see anyone in the house that night?

Dottie stated that she saw no one. She was questioned about guns. Did she or David own one? She stated that she never owned a gun, but that her husband might have owned one, but she never saw one in his possession. She further stated that she didn't know one end of a gun from another, and in all her life, never shot one, as her father did all the shooting in her family.

Her attorney now questioned her. He asked her again about a gun.

"No," she said empathically.

Did she hear a gunshot as she was running down the stairs or on the street, running away?

"No, I heard nothing except the beating of my heart," and then she broke down into huge wracking sobs. After a few minutes, she gained her composure and that is when Bateman, her attorney, asked her, "Where is the notebook, Dottie? What happened to it?"

"It's here," Dottie remarked. "Agent Brian Nedo has it in his possession. He will give it to the court."

The judge looked squarely in Nedo's direction.

"Mr. Nedo, how pleasant to see you. I assume you have the document with you?" she asked.

"Yes, your honor," said Nedo.

"And I assume you have copies for your office, the prosecutor's office, and the witnesses' attorneys?" queried the judge.

"Yes, your honor," said Nedo. He looked a little bemused and embarrassed. He liked Virginia, she was a nice lady; a real lady.

"Gentlemen," barked Virginia Ouderkirk, "are we set with this witness?"

"I have nothing further, your honor," said Ives.

"Nor I," said Bateman.

The judge nodded and Dottie stood up and left the box.

Chapter Seventy-One

Sandy Elliot took the stand when she was called. As she took the oath, she glanced nervously at Dottie, who smiled encouragingly at her.

"Now Miss Elliott, I need you to relate everything that you remember about the days before and after and the night that David Bowmaker died. Please don't leave anything out. Even the slightest little thing can be important here," said Ives.

He nodded for her to begin and Sandy started her story. "I was hired by David Bowmaker, Esquire, to be his secretary. I did typing, arranged his appointments for court hearings and trials and the usual tasks in any law office. I took the money and made the deposits at the bank and kept the books. It was a busy one-man law firm and there were lots of clients as well as what I began to call *no clients. No clients* were the ones that never had a name, just dropped off envelopes or money orders and so I called them client one, client two and so on. David was amused by this at first. Those numbers added up to some very important people on both sides of the law. When I realized this, at first, I was a little nervous, but I kept my mouth shut and my head down, as my father would have told me to do."

She sighed and continued, "Anyway, Bowmaker was a decent boss as bosses go. He didn't require favors from me, like so many of my other friends in the secretarial business. So, I was relieved and happy. I was very thorough in my bookkeeping and I would put the money that came into the office in the ledger, but on several occasions, I noticed that my entries for certain clients were blotted out and so I asked him directly what I should do. He told me..."

"Excuse me, who told you?" asked Ives.

"Mr. Bowmaker asked me to only put in the receipts and expenses from regular clients, not the ones who I deemed as client one, two...."

She continued, her cadence was slow and deliberate. "He won a lot of cases, some that I thought he was very ill-prepared for and again the clients were the ones a little on, for lack of a better word, the shady side of things. About a year into my employment I began to get a little antsy. Little things started happening, like the intense feeling I was being watched and occasionally one or two members of the FBI would call on Bowmaker just as we were closing up the office."

She hesitated, deep in thought, and then said, "Yes, I endured all the curses and the shouting and swearing, but never once did he raise a hand to me. I think he knew I knew a lot more than I needed to know. I tended not to dwell on the consequences of my ah...maybe not being needed anymore and therefore being abruptly terminated."

"Once, and it was a late night for me, one of the judges from the Appellate court called on him. I was visibly shocked but tried not to show it. I made a note of the visit. That is the first time I began to document the comings and goings at the office that were not to be spoken of."

Sandy reached for a glass of water, took a drink and set the glass down.

"It was a little over a year after I started work for him that I made the acquaintance of Mrs. Bowmaker. They had two daughters. They were cute little girls and Dorothy was a wonderful mother and very protective."

"And so, I began a wonderful friendship with Mrs. Bowmaker. To my surprise, one day Mr. Bowmaker came to me and asked where I was staying. He had a house for me to look at if I wanted. It was next door to their house. I was delighted and so was Dottie.

Dottie did tell me about the huge piles of cash in the bedroom closets and the phone calls in the middle of the night. Dottie endured all the beatings and the insults he could shove at her, but I think he knew that if anything ever happened to those girls, he would have an opponent more worthy than hell itself." She sighed and continued, "I began to realize that the phone lines were tapped and so we..."

"Excuse me," said Ives. "Who is we?"

"Oh, sorry, Mr. Bowmaker and I. Every time the phone rang and it was a conversation about a cash dump, he would state he had a house closing. I would immediately know there was cash coming in. Another one we used a lot was drawing up a will and this meant that an illicit visitor would be showing up.

It was late one November afternoon and I know he had been invited to the governor's ball at the capital. He was going, but I also knew that Dot wasn't. So, with interest, I found out that he had several favors turned and sure enough, the pictures in the morning paper told it all. There he was with this big, tall bimbo on his arm. It was disgusting to me."

Sandy paused, frowned and then said, "I began with earnest to copy the ledgers and find someplace to hide them in the office. I knew they were safe there and no matter what happened, they could be accessed."

"Where did you keep the files?" asked Ives.

Sandy said, "you have most of them, I know you do, as the day before I finally left, I told you where they were."

The attorney nodded his head. "Continue," he said.

"Several weeks before the end, Mr. Bowmaker came into the office, angrier than I've ever seen him. So angry he was foaming at the mouth. That bastard, he kept shouting. Something about a stupid Federal Judge not ruling in his client's favor. I paid that bastard plenty, plenty he kept shouting. After his tirade, he slammed the door and walked out of the office. I was really shaken up. I knew he would go to Smutty's down the road, get a few and go home where he would probably take all his injustices out on Dot.

About a week before David was killed, he told me to get rid of all the files I had on any of the clients except our regular clientele. I made sure that he," Sandy looked at the prosecutor and injected, "Mr. Bowmaker heard the shredder machine going during the day, but the more files I destroyed the more nervous I became. I wanted to find a way to get to the FBI, but I knew that every step I took, I was being watched, not only by the cops but by Bowmaker's plants and the mob.

So don't ask me why I didn't. I know that I wouldn't be alive today and I don't think that either of the girls would be either." There was a collective sigh from the gallery when she made this statement.

Sandy continued. "I occasionally babysat for the Bowmaker's, especially when Dottie had to go to the store for medicine and groceries in the evening, while my boss had court or was someplace else.

But that afternoon, the afternoon he was murdered, Bowmaker left for court around four. He knew I was babysitting that night. He informed me, as he left, that I was to wait until Dottie left for her doctor's appointment, then I was to put the girls into a car that would be parked on the street in front of the house. The car would beep it's horn once and I was to escort the girls to the car. The man in the car would give me a satchel and I would hand the two girls over. I was to leave immediately after and go to my own home and stay there."

She sighed and took a deep breath, "I was numb. Shocked. I was going to say to him, this is a joke, right? But he had already turned and was out the door.

I couldn't tell anyone. If I told Dot, she would confront David and then it would be all over for both of us. I prayed, and God gave me an answer. That night when the horn beeped outside, I ignored it. I knew it would take Dottie about two hours to complete her business, as she also had to get medicine as well as her doctor's appointment. I kept... I kept thinking to myself this is all a bad dream, a very bad dream, but no way in hell was I going to see those two little girls sold, like pieces of property."

The prosecution interjected, "how did you know they were being sold, Miss Elliot?" he queried.

"Because, Mr. Ives, how in hell would you deduce two little girls being put in a car and you being handed cash," Sandy sneered and began to openly sob.

Sandy composed herself in a courtroom that was devoid of all noise and continued her story.

"I had to move, and fast," she sneered. "I bundled the two girls up and took them out the back door and into my home, where I called my brother. He lived just across town.

I told him I needed his help. No time to talk. I told him to be very careful and not to be seen going into my house.

My brother, he's a lawyer too. The plan was to have my brother take the girls to his house and after a few days, well, I'd leave with the girls."

Sandy sighed and continued.

"I got the girls to bed in the upstairs bedroom of my house. They were tired and fell asleep immediately. I crept downstairs, making sure I kept all the lights off. I didn't have long to wait. I stood just inside the foyer of my house, listening and watching.

I saw Bowmaker walking to the front steps and climbing them. He slammed the door closed. I remember, there were cars on the street I didn't recognize. Cars that looked like they didn't belong there, like cops or maybe mob. It was about eight or nine or so. A few minutes later, Mrs. Bowmaker made her way up the steps and entered the front door.

There were a few minutes of silence. It seemed like an eternity to me and then I heard this surreal, high-pitched scream. There were several shouts, some cursing and the sound of glass shattering. A lot of glass. Then, it was deathly quiet, like a tomb. No noise from the street, no cars, just silence, like time was just waiting. I waited, I don't know how long and then I saw the figure of a woman, I knew it was Dottie. I saw her run down the steps and onto the sidewalk. I remember whispering 'Go with God' as she disappeared down the street."

Sandy hung her head. Tears streamed down her face.

The prosecuting attorney stood up. "I think I would like to motion for a short recess," he said quietly.

Judge Ouderkirk banged her gavel and stated that the hearing would resume at 2:00 pm. It was now a little past noon.

Sandy shakily stood and made her way toward the first row of seats.

As Sandy approached Dottie's seat, Dottie stood and they hugged.

"I'm so sorry," whispered Sandy.

"Oh no, I'm the one who's sorry for putting my head in the sand," said Dottie.

The two women smiled at one another and turned to face two young ladies who had waited for most of their lives for this moment.

Differently Double

Chapter Seventy-Two

At two, the courtroom was packed. No one could get in or out as the hallways outside were clogged. Police cleared the halls twice and finally put up guards to keep a manageable fire egress.

Sandy took the stand once more and continued her story.

"My brother had parked on a back street and came up the back alley between the houses. He was careful. He came in the back door and waited with me in the foyer. I remember him telling me that as he came up the back stairs and into my house, he heard something that sounded like a gunshot. There was just one shot, he told me. I didn't hear a thing and so I dismissed it. It's funny that I remember it now," she mused.

"Anyway, we returned to my vantage point in the foyer and we saw men running up the stairs of the Bowmaker home. The door was open. I remember seeing one of them looking back in the direction Dottie had run, but others were joining these men now and police showed up and it was chaos."

She paused and continued. "We waited until past 3:00 am before things finally quieted down enough and it was safe to take the girls to his house. I don't know how we did it, but we did it."

The prosecutor stood and Sandy looked at him.

"I have a quick question for the witness. Just a point of clarification please."

The judge nodded her head and said, "yes, Mr. Ives."

"If the police were scoping out the house, didn't they see you go in then see you go out?"

Sandy smiled at the question. "Yes, but I went in the back. Dottie and I made sure my comings and goings at the house were as undetected as possible."

"No further questions at the moment, your honor," said Ives.

"You may continue, Miss Elliott," said the judge.

"I went to work the next morning and of course the FEDS were waiting for me at the office. They informed me of Bowmaker's death and proceeded to tear apart the office. They cleaned out the safe and all his records, including the incriminating files. I told them I didn't know anything about Bowmaker's finances, nor where Dottie had gone. I was told by my brother that word on the street was the two girls were sold to some Atlanta attorney, who in turn had a male client who wanted two little girls to play with. Sick, isn't it?" she said in disgust.

"Anyway, I endured their questions for three more days and then finally after all the evidence was turned in and they were satisfied, I left. I was afraid for my life, and I think they were also afraid for me."

She continued, "My brother dropped us off at the train station. It took several days to get from Mobile, Alabama to Indiana, where my family is from and where my mother lived. I raised the two little girls as my nieces and that was that. Deep down I knew that someday Dot would surface."

The courtroom was quiet as she said, "Sometimes doing the right thing goes above and beyond the law. I have no regrets about my actions and I sure hope that all those years ago, some of those files were used against the scum who wished to control lives for profit. It would be a shame and such a waste if they didn't."

The defense attorney rose as did the prosecution.

"I have nothing further, your honor," said Ives.

"Nor I," said the defense.

The judge nodded and Sandy stood up and left the box.

"I have two witnesses, your honor," said the defense attorney. "I would like to call FBI retired Agent Mark Mahoney to the stand."

Agent Mahoney, a large, barrel-chested man with grey hair and a mustache, stood and made his way down to the witness stand. After being sworn in, he began his story.

"I was the lead agent on the Bowmaker case and I was stationed across the street from the Bowmakers' home the night of the murder. We were assembling to formally charge the attorney with numerous crimes, many of which were felonies. I had the arrest warrant with me at the time.

I saw a woman, known to me as Mrs. Bowmaker, leave the house and a little while later a large sedan drove up to the front of the house. It was black and honked its horn and waited a few minutes. Nothing happened and it drove away.

We did get a plate number and we did follow up on it. Shortly after that, I saw David Bowmaker enter the home, followed by his wife about ten minutes later. I heard sounds of a struggle, but I wasn't sure from my vantage point that it did, in fact, come from the Bowmakers' house.

That's when I saw Mrs. Bowmaker leave the house, run down the steps and head down the street in the direction she had come from when I first saw her enter the house. She was about three houses down on the same side of the street as the house when I exited my car and signaled my team to go. This was going down. Two of my men did go after her, but she was fast and had a good start. We lost her. It is at that moment I heard the gunshot. I ran to the house, followed by more agents, who were also parked in the street."

"I heard one gunshot, just one," he stated. "When we entered the house, the foyer was littered with glass and there was Bowmaker, face down on the floor with a bullet hole in the back of his head. When the coroner came in about an hour later that's when we learned that he had also been hit in the side of the head with a blunt object. We found the blunt object to be a golf club, laying a few feet away on the floor."

"Did you notice any drawers open in any of the cabinets that lined the walls?" asked the defense.

"I wasn't looking for that sort of thing, but my partner pointed to one drawer that was in fact open. When I looked in, it was empty and it didn't have any glass in it so we assumed that the drawer was opened after the attack went down."

"Did you find anyone else in the house?" asked the defense.

"Not a soul. No one," said Mahoney.

"I have no further questions, your honor," said Craig Ives.

The judge looked at Rick Bateman. "Nothing, your Honor," he said.

~

"My last witness is Mr. George Elliott, Esquire," announced Bateman.

[251]

George Elliott rose and proceeded down the aisle that he had traversed many times before, representing various clients in Mobile. He was a short, thin man, clean-shaven with a bald pate. He was slightly stooped in appearance and walked with a cane. He had been retired from legal work these many years and now he was back in his old haunts and relishing every minute of the experience.

After the usual formalities, he began his story.

"My sister Sandy called me. I could tell she was panicked. She told me she had to get two children out of a situation immediately. She told me the house next door, David Bowmaker's house, was under surveillance and to be careful and to come in the back way. Knowing David's reputation as not the best of persons, I parked my car on the street one block over and proceeded down the back alley between the two buildings.

As I reached the top step to Sandy's house, I heard a gunshot. Just one gunshot. It was unmistakably a gunshot. Her back door was open and I went inside the house. Sandy met me in the kitchen and we both went to the foyer in the front and watched the police activity. We kept the lights off as we didn't want the girls disturbed. They were sleeping upstairs and we didn't want police visiting us."

Standing up, Ives asked, "who were the girls?"

"They were the children of Dottie and David Bowmaker," Elliott answered.

"No further questions," said Ives.

"You may continue," said the judge.

"We waited until early morning, bundled up the girls and brought them to my house. Sandy went to work the next morning and so did I. A few days later, the two girls were on the train with Sandy headed for Indiana."

George Elliott was finished with his story and exited the witness box. As he neared the defense table Sandy stood and they embraced. He smiled wanly at her and headed toward his seat.

Rick Bateman stood. "I make a motion to have all supposed charges against my client dropped as we see there would be reasonable doubt that Dorothy Bowmaker did, in fact, kill her husband with the golf club in self-defense. Furthermore, the cause of death was from a gunshot from an unknown assailant. As stated in the coroner's report, it was the gunshot to the back of the head and not the blow to the head with the golf club that killed David Bowmaker."

The judge looked at the prosecution. As Ives stood, he had a frown on his face and he was in deep thought. He scowled and said, "In light of this testimony, I concede that if this case were to go to trial there would indeed be reasonable doubt. Therefore, the prosecution will go with the motion of the defense and all charges and supposed charges to the defendant will be dropped."

"Very well gentlemen," said the judge. "This hearing is adjourned and Mr. Bateman, I assume you will have the necessary paperwork on my desk in no later than three days."

Rick Bateman smiled and nodded his head as he turned to face Dottie and hug her.

Differently Double

Epilogue

The car drove slowly past the Emeryville diner and Dottie noticed the balloons swaying in the breeze. She saw the sandwich sign on the sidewalk and the banner in the barbershop window both saying *Congratulations Dottie*. The digital signboard at the bank gave temperature and time and another message that said *Welcome Home Dottie*. Dottie was shocked. She just shook her head and began to cry.

So much had happened in such a short time. She had spent several days with her daughters and Sandy. So much was discussed and reconciled. They were visiting her in a month and she insisted that it would be the best visit she could manage. She was excited as well as a little apprehensive.

Dave pulled the car into the driveway. It was a rental he had picked up at the airport, and he had to return it to the local garage. Dottie climbed out and Eugenia came running across the lawn. She smiled at Dottie and hugged her.

"I know you're exhausted," she said, "I did put the tea kettle on and I have fresh baked cookies."

Dottie nodded and said, "let's go in and sit a moment. I need a little tea."

Eugenia smiled, grabbed Dottie's suitcase and led her up the back steps to her house.

Eugenia poured tea and sat. "The horses are all great, but they miss you," she began, "especially those two pains in the ass. We finally had to tie them in the pasture. They decided to joy amble the other day and ended up at the cafe. I think they had two dozen donuts between them and if you take into consideration all the carrots from Steve, they each gained about twenty pounds and I lost twenty keeping track of them."

Dottie was chuckling. "They keep you on your toes, don't they?"

Eugenia smiled and continued, "Mandy did great. Your students were very nice to her and gave her jobs and she's quite happy being with the horses. Ferd still supervises her and all, but I guess the more ya live, the more you learn. And boy have I learned a lot about animals and people."

"Lydia and Olivia have been cleaning out your flower beds and mowing your lawn. Kenny supervises that crew," she said.

Just then, the two women glanced out the window. They saw Valerie and Ferd standing patiently at the gate waiting.

"Well, I better give the welcoming party pats, or they'll be mad at me for weeks," said Dottie, beaming.

Both women walked out onto the porch. Then Dottie walked down her porch steps and across the yard toward the paddock. The dynamic *equine duo* greeted her with soft nickers and snorts. It was good to be home.